Gallows Humour

This book is a work of fiction. Names, characters, places, and incidents are the product of the author's imagination or are used fictitiously. Any resemblance to actual events, locales, or persons, living or dead, is coincidental.

'til there's nothing left to burn and nowhere to run.

-        The Glorious Sons

1

The Gravedigger and The Boot

True Gallows dug graves. It was their way of paying respect to the dead bodies they robbed, and it helped to relieve the overall rotting-ness of the ruined prairie cities they scavenged in. They enjoyed the labour, as much as a person could enjoy that kind of labour. Robbing bodies, digging graves. It was honest work. Sort of. Kept them fit, kept them fed. They had gotten good at it.

Plus, people left them alone. Scavengers like True travelled on their own, or in the smallest of polycules. Pickings were too slim, trust was too low, and infighting got lethal fast. Civilians kept their distance from scavengers for the most part. And whenever a warm body slinked up to True in the waning hours of the After Market, they made sure to pull down their tattered blue bandana and let everyone get a good eyeful of the canyon scar splitting their face from tooth to eye.

They patted the final clods of dirt onto a mound. Second of the day. Straightening, they stretched sore muscles and squinted at the blushing evening sky. They'd had a late start. One more grave would push them into dark hours. On the other hand, the first two corpses hadn't yielded a satisfactory harvest. With a reluctant frown, they clipped their shovel to their pack. They could picture every bit of loot nestled deep inside it: A handful of cheap costume jewelry, sure to turn some travelling performer's neck green; surprisingly unrotted teeth pulled from the slack mandible of a blue corpse; and even dentures from the decrepit old lady they'd just buried. The dentures were a real prize. Almost sufficient to make up for how terrible the rest of the scavenge had gone.

They sniffled, and a foul expression crumpled their face. It was bad enough they had a crater for a nose, it had to be leaky, too. Fucking allergies.

They turned their back on the graves and stomped off towards the street. Best not risk losing daylight to a third grave, or drawing the shadow dwellers out with a late evening pyre. They could stand a couple leans nights. That was nothing new.

Shadows unfurled over the mid-summer prairie heat. When the sun set, the cities became hunting grounds for the night creatures and the dwellers, and only the incredibly stupid set foot on the crumbled asphalt with them. Nothing made True's skin crawl quite like those creepy denizens of the dark. Sure, True stole from dead people, but they never ate anyone.

They clomped down the road. Couldn't sneak half as well as the shadow dwellers, puffing up all loud and scary was the next best option.

The sky deepened from rust orange to bruise purple. Stars began to twinkle warnings above the decomposing city. True vaguely remembered a time when streetlights blotted out the stars. A lifetime ago, before all the people operating and paying for the lights died or went nuts.

"You're out late."

Speaking of nuts.

"You're out early," True said back, watching the shadow dweller out of the corner of their eye. They swept the surrounding debris, keyed up and ready to bolt at the first sign of motion. A single dweller wasn't unmanageable, but dwellers tended to travel in packs.

Nothing yet. Back to the shadow dweller trailing after them. Pale, wiry, small. Eyes gleaming with malice and hunger. It wasn't dressed that different from True; an oversized coat with more pockets than empty space, long pants, heavy boots. True wore a dark blue wool sash cinched around their waist, and the bandana over their face, of course, but they thought the bigger difference was the way the dweller held itself. Hunched over, so its knobby spine poked up beneath its coat.

They wondered if it was doing that on purpose, or if its body was halfway through a slow and morbid death. A bug curling up on itself. Harrowing sorts of diseases thrived in the shadow communities. Brutal things that ate their victims from the inside, scraping at their brains the way the shadow dwellers scraped at the brains of the people they cannibalized. Some called it retribution. True called it creepy. And dangerous, the sick ones were a hell of a lot wilder.

Hints of sickness clung to the dweller. It was a deep-cave-creature shade of pale compared to True's sun-cooked brown. Its hair tangled with the rot that stuck to the bottom of ditches, where True's, while slick with grease, was at least finger-combed and sort of cut. As much cut as a rusty pair of garden shears could get it. They'd given their ears a wide berth, wary of the clumsy blades, but they'd been determined to do it. Shorter hair was easier to deal with. Harder to grab fistfuls of, didn't flop in the way as much.

"Dangerous, wandering all alone at night," the dweller said. It had to leap every few steps to keep up with True's quick gait. Snot trickled down the dweller's chin. True had heard tales of one sickness that dissolved the brain until it sloughed out the nose, but they found a more accurate tell was the way the dweller's eyes juddered, dizzying and uncontrollable.

"Dangerous," True repeated, their lisp clinging to the end of the word. The shadow dweller snickered.

"Can't even talk proper."

The carabiner clicked as True unclipped the shovel from their pack. Step—pivot—*crunch*. They swung the shovel straight into the dweller's face. It crumpled like a marionette with snipped strings and True turned back to the road.

That was enough of that.

Flp. They froze, midstep. Murderous annoyance clouded their fragmented features as they took another testy step.

Sk-flp. Thin rubber slapped the bottom of their foot. Glaring down at their boot, they lifted it. The sole flopped down towards the dirt, that pivot had been the last straw for the twine they'd tied the offending footwear together with. Now the sad rubber clung on by a heel. Scrunching up their face, they flipped their useless shoe the bird. Perfect, those couple of lean nights had just stretched into a week, at least.

The moon climbed higher in the evening sky, and they set off again, *sk-flping* down the highway.

2
The After Market

The After Market bustled to life at dusk in the wake of the usual trade day, stretching like a cat. Skittish like one, too, always skulking around the underbellies of cities with both eyes peeled. Sandwiched between the dreary hours of dusk and witching hour. In daylight, the degrading cities were pocked with markets and passing caravans. Civilians and merchants traded amongst each other. Food, clothes, trinkets, medicines, passed from hand to hand. But things got used up or worn down, and there were precious few people left with the skills to make new supplies. More now than there had been at the peak of the starvation years, but not sufficient to keep up with demand, yet.

That was where scavengers and the After Market vendors came in. They went places no one else was willing to go, they took things no one else was willing to take, and as long as they were quiet about it, nobody turned up any noses when fresh material appeared in the trade stream.

Almost nobody.

True narrowed their eyes at a medic symbol, the sign of the Red Faction, spray-painted to the face of a crumbled garden wall. The red paint had drooled down the brick in places, whoever had plastered it there had held the spray can too close to the surface. Those things were getting uncomfortably close to this city's After Market.

All are welcome. Read a line of oozy paint under the symbol.

Except scavengers, True corrected it in their head as they passed by. A factioneer would sooner catch black lung than offer their medical service to a scavenger.

It was less of a rumour and more of an open secret that the Red Faction abhorred scavenging and thought everyone else should, too. It was *dirty.* Yeah, well, the dead weren't complaining and there were way more corpses than factioneers to defend them. Though Faction presence had been infiltrating deeper into the prairies the past few months. Deeper into True's territory.

Must be nice, True thought, to have the food and clothing to consider the After Market optional.

Five blocks later, they ducked down a narrow alley and emerged in a tiny paracosm of dozens of ramshackle merchant stalls. Sickly kerosene lamps offered low light, the tiny flames wavering in anticipation of being extinguished at the first sign of trouble. True's shoe sole *sk-flped* carelessly in the wind. Their loot bag, now retrieved from deep inside their pack and fastened to their belt, bounced on their thigh. Hushed conversation hummed in the air, a dull buzz in True's ear. Most people tried to keep the noise down, what with it being a secret black market and all, but there were simply too many people for it to be quiet.

After an age and a half *sk-flping* though the lean After Market crowd, they made it to the vendor they'd come for. Finally. They crouched, and, popping back up, strode to the makeshift counter. Their boots hit the pressboard with a resounding thunk, mud flaked off onto the tired cloth. Before the last flake had drifted to its resting place, the vendor had peeked once, twice, her beady eyes locked onto them, at once gleaming with fury.

"You get those mucky atrocities off my table, True." She descended on them with a hawkish sneer, shoving the boots off. True snagged them before they hit dirt. They paused while the scavengers the vendor had been chatting up figured out how to shut their gaping maws.

"I need new ones," they said, dropping the boots back on the counter.

"Too bad," the vendor snapped, spittle flying from her gummy mouth. Fixing them with a glower, she pushed the boots off and turned back to rescue her conversation with her other patrons. Unfazed, True drew the dentures from their sack and set them on the counter, hard. The fake teeth clacked. It worked like a charm. The vendor's ears practically twitched. True lifted their hand, giving her a good look at their prize, and waited out her routine feigning of disinterest. She sucked her lone, grey front tooth, producing a sort of squeaky wet fart noise as any part of her lip not supported by the tooth flapped. Then, continued her conversation. But True saw the way her check quivered from the effort of not snatching up those shiny new teeth.

"Galya," they said. She pointedly ignored them and gummed the inside of her hollow cheek. True smirked. They had her. Pocketing the dentures, they waited for the other customers to wander away with their own goods traded and pocketed.

"I've said it before, and I'll say it again. You're a shit barterer, True."

"I get what I need," True replied. Knocking their old boots, they grumbled, "hurry up, it's too cold for bare feet."

It was Galya's turn to snicker. Thin lips stretched into a shrewish pretense of a grin.

"Gimme those chompers."

"Boots first."

Her withered head ducked under the counter, where she made a show of shuffling her crates of junk around. As if size ten shoes were hard to find.

Fog began to roll in, choking out the flickering lamps. A pair strolled by, scavengers, judging by the size of their packs. One too tall, too pale, and with a delicate bone structure at odds with their enormous muscled stature. The other scavenger was more compact, with darker colouring and a streak of white sprouting from her forehead. It could have been the dim, unreliable light, but both scavengers looked clean. A revelation that made True take a second gander. Sure, they both had limp, greasy hair and stained clothes, but where was the permadirt that outlined every crease on everyone else?

The shorter one scanned True once and again with suspicious eyes. Lingering first on their bare feet, then on their bandana. True let her catch their glare and held it until she leaned into her partner and muttered something. Nosy bastards. They adjusted their bandana.

"Pay up." Galya dropped her ware on the counter, rattling the unstable construct. Dismayed, True picked up the lone, brown work boot by its frayed laces.

"Where's the other?"

"That's all I have." She splayed her fingers, palms up, as if to say 'what can ya do.'

"Bull," True grumbled, "the dentures are worth more than a pair. I'm giving you the best trade you'll get all month and you're ripping me off,"

Galya scoffed. Fuming, True flung the boot at her and stalked away.

"Where ya goin' in bare feet, nutbag?" Galya shouted after them.

"To trade with a hag who won't cheat me!"

"Nobody else wants your dirty stolen dentures."

"Wanna bet?" They stuck a middle finger high for her to see. Of course, they kept finding reasons to wander through her city. She never stared, she didn't flirt, and she'd been a vendor as long as True had been a scavenger, which was to say, long enough to be familiar. They made it a few more good strides before Galya called again.

"I'll give you licorice."

True slowed to a stop. They tongued the point of their canine, daring to waffle. The crowd creeped in on their unmoving body.

"I got a whole bag," crowed Galya.

A few stomps later and they were back at her counter.

"At least give me one that matches my other boot."

Galya pulled an old, crumpled chip bag from the depths of her bottomless apron pockets and laid it on the cloth beside the boot.

"Don't got any others in your size," she said. Swiping the licorice, True tossed the dentures overhand.

"This is extortion."

Galya snatched the dentures from the air. "Pick words you can pronounce."

"Bitch."

"Yeah, like that one."

Yanking on their newly mismatched boots, True tromped off into the fog and unwashed bodies to trade the rest of their harvest to someone who would afford them the usual ogling and pinched lips instead of Galya's overfamiliar bullying. She never failed to ruffle their feathers, like they were a damn chicken. Stupid extortionist vendor.

"True!"

They ignored her.

"You look skinny, eh? Come back more often so I know you don't starve."

They turned back one last time to touch their fingertips to their head. That stupid extortionist vendor also happened to be the closest thing to a friend True had left.

No more *sk-flp* at least.

3
The Ragamuffin

Another day, another street full of dead bodies. True jimmied the lock on the front door of the first house on a pathetic little cul-de-sac. It was faster to smash a window, but it was also louder, and they'd been carting around a bad gut feeling all day. With the creak and shudder of hinges that had forgotten their purpose, the door yielded.

Inside, the house told a story True had read a thousand times. A broken coatrack laying on the floor, papers strewn across the office, and the empty shells of eviscerated electronics left to gather thick layers of dust wherever they had been tossed by second wave raiders. True ran a finger over a dent in the drywall, a landline phone lay on the hardwood beneath it.

Every once in a while it hit them that this had all happened in their lifetime. That the most horrifying part of the black lung had been how fast it razed the planet and obliterated everyone's way of life. If they cared to, they could picture their old life almost perfectly. Their severance from it had been so abrupt that it felt like an alternate reality, sealed off from the dry-rot of time.

But they didn't care to. That door could stay shut.

They moved through the kitchen, where cabinets had been flung open. The fridge had been left wide open, a carpet of green and black coated the insides and the floor around it and speckled the wall. A bit of pink plastic from the milk jug that had detonated and given the mold splatter life poked out of the slime. They left the kitchen untouched. First wave scavengers would have cleaned out anything useable, no point disturbing that brand new ecosystem.

They cut through a living room with a couch that looked like mouse central, and into a hallway that had lonely nails jutting out where pictures had once hung. All the doors branching from the hall stood wide open, except one.

Bingo. Families always left the door closed. Maybe out of respect, but probably out of guilt. Nobody wanted to watch, or be watched by, a dying loved one while hurrying to abandon them. True hesitated at the mouth of the hall, their skin prickling with apprehension. Nothing in the infested living room except the rodents. No flickers of motion in the windows or the kitchen doorway. They were alone. They pressed their tongue to their canine. Just them and the corpse, and the sprouting civilization in the kitchen. They turned their attention back to the closed door.

A gust of warm wind hustled out of the room in the wake of the door opening. Lime green walls glowed out of the gloom. Stickers had been stuck at random on the wall, the game console stashed in the corner, the lamp on the bedside table. True had the decency to pause when they saw the shelf of children's toys. But not for long. Kids died. True had to eat. They couldn't make it better, they could only make the best of the aftermath.

This one was tidy, at least. Surprisingly so. As if someone had come in after the passing to clean up the usual mess. An unopened bottle of water and two neatly stacked granola bars had been set beside the door. Loved ones left final gifts like that often. Tokens of hope that the person in the room might somehow regain the strength to flee. They never did.

True ignored the instinct to grab those precious commodities. They had made the mistake of drinking from a sealed death room water bottle, once. They'd spent the next week on the brink of death, shitting their brains out. So, it was safe to say they weren't keen on trying again anytime soon. Those tokens were cursed.

They opened the blinds to let the light in and check for any nosy problems outside. The coast remained clear. So far.

Alright, well, time for the corpse then.

Someone—a parent probably—had tucked it in with blankets up to its nose. None of the usual blood splatter from coughing out liquidated lung tissue stained the wall. Signs of the end stages of the disease that had decimated the planet were not subtle. It wasn't like the shadow dweller sicknesses that slowly hollowed people out until only a thin husk persisted. The black lung had snapped victims up and shaken the life out of them, quick and violent.

So, what, had the family tucked in a dead body?

True's gaze fell on the bottles stacked on the bedside table. They picked up the orange prescription bottle first, pleased to hear it rattle. Its label read azithromycin. Jackpot. They'd make a fortune off this, everyone and their cat wanted antibiotics. They shoved it deep in their loot bag, then, on second thought, they took it out and tucked it into a secret inner pocket of their well-worn coat. Best to keep those close, other scavengers would kill for bottle of pills.

They checked the other bottle too. Cough syrup, adult strength. Empty. The label looked as new as anything did these days. Suddenly the mystery of the über tidy death room became clearer.

Setting the cough syrup down, True pinched a corner of the sheets and lifted. The blanket crackled as it peeled from mouth of the corpse, its grey decaying skin sloughing with it in chunks. There was the last piece of that puzzle.

Dried vomit of a strange purple hue stuck to everything from the nose to the collarbones. The kid hadn't even turned its head, it had probably been knocked out by the cold medicine. It was kind of a peaceful way to die, at least for a kid. Mommy gives you an icky drink and tucks you in and then you just fall asleep. Wouldn't even hurt. Not how True would pick to go out, but they weren't a child.

They checked the corpse's ears for jewelry and found nothing in the dried-up remnants of the lobes. No pockets on the pajamas. They unstuck the mouth and pulled the jaw open. Decay had released the body from rigor mortis long since, rendering it pliable and fragile. They had to be careful with how they moved things, or parts were liable to break. Gently, they rubbed the purple stain from the molars. No evidence of fillings. Too bad, there was nothing else to harvest from the body. They gave the rest of the room a once-over but came up empty-handed. Children's rooms rarely had many tradeable goods. Oh well, the azithro more than made up for this empty room, and the next few to come.

They retrieved a sheet from the unmade bed in the master bedroom, shook out the evidence of critter life, and laid it on the corpse's bedroom floor. Again, while they crouched over the sheet, that bad gut feeling bubbled to the surface. Stronger than before. They reached for their shovel. Steady, steady.

No one at the window.

They unclipped the shovel. A floorboard creaked. True sprang like a startled cat, whirling to face the sound, swinging their shovel about with them.

The intruder stumbled back, missing the knife edge of the shovel by a hair. True glared down the shovel handle at the unflapped mass of blackened rags and sad eyes. Sighing, they lowered the shovel.

"Damn it, Radio, I told you to quit creeping around."

The pile of rags grinned.

"Told you to quit following me, too."

It shrugged, earning itself an irritated eye roll.

Radio, short for Radio Silent—which wasn't its name, probably, but it was so damn quiet all the time. It was a dogged little shit, too. True had slipped off in increasingly precarious ways, the last time even slinking away in the most dangerous hour of the day, right before the sun rose, in hopes of giving it the slip.

Scavengers sometimes spawned schools of other vultures. Remoras that followed them around and fed off the algae under the scavenger's fins. Some scavengers ignored them, some chummed the water for them, but True preferred to stomp on their little fish heads and scare them off.

This is my loot, don't you try and take it." True lifted the shovel again in warning. Not that Radio ever touched their stuff, and its eyes didn't dance, and it didn't wear a medic patch, which meant True refrained from whacking it over the head. But man, they were over the stalking. They returned to finish their task. Talk about a mood killer. How many more times were they gonna have to dodge that fucker before it got the hint? They worked alone, and for good reason: Everyone left on the planet sucked fat donkey balls. The end.

By mid-evening True had nine bodies in sheets stacked neatly in the middle of the cul-de-sac and their loot bag weighted with a half-decent haul. They'd managed to clear out all the houses while Radio shuffled around in the background doing whatever Radio did. The decision to build a pyre instead of digging graves meant they had time to scavenge more and make up for yesterday's denture rip-off.

They finished opening the last of the death room tokens they had found and set it with the others on a square of tinfoil that they had pinched into the shape of a plate; a meal for the ones that had gone ahead. Laying the plate on the pyre, they plucked their trusty lighter from their right coat pocket.

They'd traded a hefty amount for it, much to their chagrin at the time. It even lit in heavy wind! Or so the hawker who had sold it to them had claimed. True never lit fires on windy days because they weren't a moron.

Sparking a mellow flame, they appreciated it for a moment before touching it to a corner of a bedsheet. It took slowly. They had no fuel to encourage it, but it would burn fine once it caught. They stood while the flames stretched their tongues over the sheets, letting the heat drag claws over their skin, letting the light pinch their pupils, letting gusts of heat whistle through the tassels of their sash and dry their tongue. The same heat rustled Radio Silent's Kainai beaded poncho as appeared to their left, just outside of shovel reach.

The two of them watched the flames eat the corpses, burn and burn and burn.

The sky was taking on its first wisps of midnight blue by the time the fire chewed everything into a pile of brittle ash. Chalky white bone dust glowed in places where the embers clung to life. True smoothed their bandana and turned from the remains. Something—or rather, someone—snagged their sleeve. They jerked away.

"Hands off, ya little creep."

Radio jabbed its finger across the ash pile, where moving shadows bobbed towards the cul-de-sac. True frowned, reaching for their shovel. It was early for shadow dwellers.

"Alright, come on," they whispered, reluctantly beckoning for Radio to follow them as they snuck to the nearest house. "Try to be quiet, if you can."

Ha, such a funny joke.

At the sunken corner of a dilapidated porch the hunkered down. Radio shrank into the shadows behind them. The shadow dwellers made good time, strolling past the mouth of the cul-de-sac while the grass settled around True's coat. True pressed their hand to the remnants of their nose and rolled their eyes skyward, willing a sneeze to evaporate. If they just held their breath, the dwellers would pass, and they could sneak off in the opposite direction.

"Told you I saw a fire," a woman's voice said, followed by the scrape and skitter of something light being kicked across the road. True blinked back tears in time to see the charred clump of tinfoil skid to a halt at the curb, ash puffed into the air. Disrespectful assholes.

Four in total lingered in the midst of the ashes. A curly-haired man, a blond giant, a weasel in yellow shoes, and the woman who had spoken, who was now skimming the cul-de-sac in a slow circle.

"All this work we put into building a new world and they're out here determined to feed off the scraps of the old one. Like maggots." She faked a gag. Just for a second, the dying sunlight hit the streak of white sprouting from her crown and recognition pinched True's gut. She'd been at the After Market last night, and blondie, too.

True's blood simmered as they forced a slow, controlled breath out. They should have known those two were snakes, they'd been too clean. Only factioneers were that antiseptic.

"Someone's morbid today," the curly-haired guy said.

"Shut up, Heath," the woman snapped.

"And touchy, *Otsana*."

"I said shut up."

"Make—" his sentence ended in an abrupt squawk when the giant hoisted him by the back of his neck.

"Apologize," the giant rumbled. Curly thrashed, face reddening.

"I'm not apologizing 'cause your girlfriend's scared she's gonna screw up and cost us a market," he snarled, doing his best to sound intimidating and indignant in spite of the spit bubbling at the corners of his mouth and the way the punch he threw bopped uselessly off the giant. The giant lowered him until his feet stood flat on the ground, just in time for the woman to nail him in the beans. He folded with a guttural groan and the giant let him land with his full weight.

"It's wife," the woman corrected, "and I'm never scared. Get up, we're going to be late."

Lacing her fingers through the giant's, she led them out of the ash pile. Curly staggered to his knees, the sweat on his brow forming a grey paste with the ash. Huffing and puffing, he hobbled after the rest of his group.

"You dickheads can't be married, there's no damn priests left," he grumbled.

The weasel chimed in then, his voice fading with the distance. "I thought Miranda..."

At last, the factioneers were out of earshot. True threw themself from the grass, smothering a sneezing fit that felt like the gates of hell had opened in their nasal passage and unleashed the unholiest of brimstone.

When they recovered, they were alone.

Yeah, right. Wishful thinking. Radio had just turned itself into a poltergeist again, or however it managed to always be there but never in their eyeline. They were tired of getting spooked by it.

Grumbling silently to themself, they unhooked their shovel and trudged away. The night sank into their warm skin, creeping into their heart and lungs. Pollen itched their sinuses. Debris crunched under their mismatched shoes, they avoided what they could but for the most part they had to focus on not tripping and impaling themself on a rusty deck nail. Priorities, priorities.

A pack of feral dogs sang their commitments to the rising moon, announcing the death of the last vestige of sunlight. It was a while yet before the derelict townhouse came into sight, and with it, a tooth-grinding view. Luck was not on their side.

Around the back of the house, signs of life had sprung up, they were not the only person who had scouted this place.

A twig snapped. True flinched. It was stupid to be out at night like this. They skimmed the other houses; broken windows, a front door hanging off its hinges, a roof caved in by a dead fallen tree. All things they had noticed the first time they'd strolled through, all things that made those houses shitty places to hole up. What was the point of hiding inside if all the outside could come in?

They gambled another handful of seconds out in the open, then followed a fresh-stomped path through the overgrown grass to a basement window, propped open by a brick. Even in an already occupied house, they had better chances inside than out. At least inside didn't have roving packs of feral cats.

The window could fit a person, but not a person and a pack. They'd have to drag it in after them, and risk leaving themself open to attack. Or they could push it in first, alert the stranger to the presence, and let them snag all True's earthly possessions in one go. Yeah, no. Potential stab in the back it was.

They hesitated with their hand on their strap. There were other paths in the grass, fresh, the flattened stalks groaning back upright. They didn't like the way the paths came from all different directions to converge on the window. A civilian group would have come all in one.

Abandoning their invasion plan, they eased themself down by the window and peered in. The glass, clouded with dust and dirt, revealed little more than moving blobs. Two, six... at least eight. Low voices filtered through the gap. They leaned closer to eavesdrop.

Muttering. They caught a few nonsensical snippets as the mutterers' volume rose and ebbed or one of them passed under the window. Hunting, being hunted, blue, foxes, evil computers.

There was a pause coloured by rustling, inside and out. True's attention snapped to the outside world. Specifically, to the ragamuffin in black settling into the grass on the opposite side of the window. Radio pressed its finger to its mouth. True made a note to yell at it later and send it packing for good. Later. They put their ear to the gap again.

Definitely shadow dwellers.

Shit. True mouthed the word, then, like the punchline of the world's worst prank show, they sneezed. Conversation inside the basement cut off abruptly. Fucking *allergies.*

Double shit. They punted the brick propping the window open. The brick had barely kissed the ground by the time they had taken off. A second set of footsteps pattered after them. Radio, lighter and fleeter by far, caught up with ease. Roaring sprang out of the house, chasing after them.

True put their head down and threw themself into a run toward the heart of the city. Toward the After Market. It was too late to hide, they needed the safety of other armed people.

Hot breath chased chills down their spine.

True peaked the summit of a hill overlooking the walking bridge between two hollowed skyscrapers that marked the main entrance of the After Market. Sweat ran into their eyes, and a force like a locomotive slammed them to the pavement. They lost skin skidding downhill. Elbows locked, holding the lunatic shadow dweller away from their face. They landed on their back, the shadow rat thunking its full weight onto them. It sank its teeth into True's arm.

Cursing, True tried and failed to flip it. Their own blood waterfalled into their mouth.

As suddenly as the shadow dweller had hit them, a black figure slammed into it. True rolled to their knees too fast, the weight of their pack penduluming them hard.

"Hold it!" they bellowed. Hands met shovel met skull. The shadow dweller squelched. No more shadow dweller. True rocked back on their haunches, wiped the blood from their mouth. Five seconds, they could have five seconds to catch their breath.

Five.

Their blood made their mouth taste of rusted copper.

Four.

It was probably only their blood, they hadn't hit the shadow dweller that hard for blood to splatter all the way up to their mouth.

Three.

Their scalp burned where it had scraped on the pavement. That would smart for a while.

Two.

Remember to breathe now.

One.

Exhale. They got to their feet. Popped Radio on the shoulder. "Get up. The Market."

Radio clambered off the dead shadow dweller's knees and sauntered after True.

"I didn't need your help." True said.

Radio said nothing.

"Are you deaf or just—"

An inconveniently timed explosion tore the end of their sentence to dust. Which was nothing compared to the eyeball-searing flash and a second wave that wiped out everything in its path, True included.

Skin, seared. Ears, ringing like church bells. Head, felt like a dumbass had packed it with jelly instead of brains. True peeled themself off the concrete, blinking away blurriness. They patted their pack straps to make sure it was there, smoothed their bandana in place. Wiggled all ten fingers, all nine toes. They'd ended up a good car length farther up the hill from where they'd started. And there, below, were the burning remnants of the After Market.

What in unholy hell.

Movement among the flames caught their eye. A shape made its way out of the blast zone, limping. There were people alive down there. True pushed themself upright and staggered downhill.

The heat of the fires rushed up to meet them, kissing all the same places the pyre had mere hours earlier. They reached the bottom of the hill just in time to watch a towering shape leap from a hidden corner and take the limping shape to the ground. Firelight reflected off the giant's pale skin. True ducked behind the shell of a car. Hiding. Deliberating.

That hadn't been a shadow dweller. And that sure as hell didn't look like healing.

The ringing in their ears began to give way to crackles from the flames, screams, and the occasional whoop. The shadow dwellers *they* led here taking advantage of an opportunity to pick off lightly barbequed stragglers. They uncurled from their hiding spot, shovel gripped in hand, and jogged into the fire.

Their feet carried them through the familiar streets, now lit up by destruction in place of kerosene lamps. Bodies littered the streets between decimated tables and ashy remnants of trades. Deeper in, the bodies looked more like hamburger than people. Roaring fire and the sounds of agony replaced the church bells in their ears. Not much of an upgrade. They found the mangled street they were looking for, too close to the gutted core of the blast for hope, and yet they couldn't convince themself to walk away.

"Galya!" they called. Her counter was a wreck, half of it crushed under the collapsed wall of the building it had nestled beside. Plaster dust and black smoke choked the air. They coughed, ducking under the smoldering lumber. "Galya!"

A horrid moan drew their attention to a debris-crowded corner.

She was mangled like her street. One leg visibly broken, the exposed skin on her arms yellow with bloated blisters. True kneeled beside her. Warm blood soaked their pants. There was a lot of it, they couldn't see where it came from. In fact, they were having a hard time looking at anything except the canyon stretching from ear to gored eye socket. Splinters of wood and bone mingle in the torn flesh.

"You're stupider than I thought." She reached up to rap their head. They could only watch in helpless horror as her intestines, no longer held in by her arm, spilled. Oh, that's where the blood was from.

"You're the one who got herself killed," they said. Galya rasped out a death-rattle-esque laugh and True tried not to stare at the way it made her intestines dance and writhe.

"Let me save you the trouble of harvesting me."

"Don't—"

But she was already lifting her other deformed arm to press something heavy and too warm to their chest. A handgun. True's eyes widened. Who the hell had guns these days? True knew how to shoot. A BB gun. The real thing was different. Loud, heavy, hard to manage, not worth the practice.

"Kill the bastards that did this, eh, True?" Galya said, an unreadable gleam in her remaining eye. Her hand fell from the gun. A swollen blister burst on impact, spraying them both with sticky plasma. She yelped, and just like that, went dim. Slack-faced, blank-stared, chest stilled.

Tucking the gun into their waistband, they reached up with bare hands to wrench a burning chunk of lumber free from the debris and touched the flames to Galya. Smoke stung their eyes as they walked away.

4
The Coffin Room

The last thing they wanted was to spend the night out in the open. The last thing, after staying the night in town. They made it to the outskirts of the city ruins, the Market an orange glow at their back. Their arm throbbed and their palms stung where they hadn't been careful with the burning debris. More than that, they were tired. Deep tired. Muscle weighing too heavy on bone.

By a stroke of luck, they stumbled upon a farmhouse just off the abandoned highway beyond the rusted power plants that marked the edge of the city. It wasn't the safest place to lay, but it was better than nothing. True walked in. The door wasn't even locked. Country folk were like, before they all died. Not a lot of break-and-enter type crime out in the sticks.

They shunted the bolt shut behind them and straggled through a cursory check of the house.

Empty. Empty. Empty. No shadow dwellers, no factioneers, no bodies. The basement was either nonexistent or hidden behind a locked hall door that they couldn't be bothered to dig up a key for. They scrounged a blanket out of the linen closet and retreated to the master bedroom to lick their wounds. The bed called to them. Fluffy, rumpled blankets looking practically luxurious. They dropped their salvaged blanket on the carpet and killed the desire to crawl onto the giant, comfy mattress with the reminder that someone had probably died on it and oozed into the springs.

Pack unclipped, thumping to the floor next to the tokens. They stuck the gun deep in the bottom. Old coat, shrugged off. They rolled up their ragged sleeve to inspect the damage there. It looked better than it felt. A crescent of welts decorated it top and bottom, but their coat had borne the brunt of the bite. The blood had come from a small, jagged puncture on the soft belly of their wrist, from a shard of glass or a loose nail when they'd hit the ground. Which was a more horrible way to die, they wondered, rabies or tetanus? They fished out their meager first aid supplies.

Half an old baby food jar of salve and a dwindled supply of gauze wrap. They smeared a thin layer of salve over the bloodied patches of their skin and the burns on their calloused palms. They wrapped the blisters in hopes of protecting them from bursting, and the last of their precious gauze went to the seeping wrist puncture. Coat on back. Blanket around shoulders. They rested their head on their pack and blinked up at the bed until an uneasy sleep fell over them.

Suffocating pressure startled them awake, and realization seized their sleep-addled brain.

There were no bodies.

Replaced at once by the instinct to throw the weight pinning them down. Hissing. A beat of struggle passed while their eyes adjusted and their brain overrode their fight or flight to register Radio's caliginous form.

Hushing, not hissing.

True grabbed its wrists and tore it off.

"What the fuck are you doing?" they demanded. How had it even gotten in? It scuttled away and rolled under the bed. Hiding now? They reached. The door slammed open, straight into True's face, deleting the next several seconds from existence. They blinked back to life with a mouth full of blood and splitting headache.

They dove for their shovel only for it to be kicked out of reach by a pair of ugly yellow sneakers. The doorslammer grabbed a fistful of their hair and yanked them to their knees.

"Look at this little rat," the doorslammer gave them a shake. Asshole. They spied the red medic patch on his shoulder and recognized the weaselly form of one of the factioneers from earlier that night. True punched him in his weasel schnozz. Blood sprayed, True's knuckles smarted almost as much as their scalp. Doorslammer swore viciously, dropping True. It gave them a few precious seconds. They snatched their shovel from the corner, swung. And froze at the razor-sharp edge of a makeshift spear pressed to their throat. The curly-haired factioneer stood in the door, looking down the spear with dead eyes, as if he could slide the blade into True's gullet and watch them choke to death on the end of it without blinking. Best not test that theory. They dropped their shovel.

"Smart," Spear said. "On your feet."

"Hey!" Doorslammer lurched deeper into the room. True could only watch with clenched teeth as the factioneer crammed his broad shoulders under the bed and re-surfaced dragging Radio.

Great, now they were both dead.

The factioneers marched them out of the bedroom. The reek of smoke clogged the air, feeding True's dread. A door banged shut in the kitchen with a force that rattled the abandoned picture frames on the hallway wall. Doorslammer shoved Radio into the kitchen, it's toes catching on the lip of the tile.

A short woman stood before the shut kitchen door, fingers drumming on the counter. Scorch marks glowed on her arms, soot stained the white streak in her hair and streaked her red cheeks.

"Done kissing your boyfriend goodbye?" Doorslammer asked. Sneered, more like. Otsana slammed her fist on the counter, whipping about. Doorslammer squeaked Radio into her path in his place in the nick of time. With an audible thump her fist sank into Radio's gut. Doorslammer let it drop. It curled with a limp heave that True didn't make sense of until a wet splatter hit the tile. Morbidly, True envied the ability to puke silently. Less morbidly, they noticed the only stuff coming out of it was highlighter yellow bile. No wonder it had tripped on that non-existent tile ledge. It hadn't eaten in a while.

"Don't take your bad mood out on me," Doorslammer said, dodging Otsana's next swipe.

"Hrōkr is my *spouse*, bitch."

"You and your spouse—" he drew it out mockingly "—fucked our chance at the market."

Doorslammer rounded on True, shoving them into a kitchen chair. They dropped out of range of the spear, but zip-ties snapped tight around their wrists.

"Did you like Otsana's fireworks show, scavenger?" He jostled the chair arm. Grabbing True's face, he squeezed and swivelled them to face Otsana. Spear was busy flopping Radio into a second kitchen chair.

"How was I supposed to know there was propane in that basement?"

"Did you check?" Spear chimed in. Otsana turned an evil eye on him. He caved much easier than Doorslammer.

"At least the night isn't a complete loss. Don't worry we'll make more use of you and your friend than we did of your crispy-fried market buddies."

True bit their tongue, gasoline percolating in their gut. The weaselly factioneer seemed to notice and relish in it. He smacked them upside the head on his way past.

"This one has a nasty glare on her," he said.

True graced him with the full glory of their nasty glare, unfortunately he was halfway down the hall.

"Her? You think?" Doorslammer pulled them up by their hair. Their achy scalp was on the verge of peeling off. Otsana settling her hip on the counter, a glower on her smoke-stained features. She flicked her fingers noncommittally over True.

"Hard to tell with that junk on their face."

For the first time that night, True flinched, away from the factioneer reaching for their bandana. To no avail. The bandana came off in one fell tug and then it was the factioneers' turn to flinch. Otsana's lip curled, revulsion plain on her face.

The doorslammer scoffed. "Shit, dude, can you even speak with a face like that?"

"Fuck you," they said with as much venom as they could muster. His knuckles cracked across True's face, snapping their head to the side. Their vision sparked. They found their way back to Otsana's sullen gaze. Her haughty attitude wavered for a brief second her eyes shifted and her arms folded tighter over herself. Good, she should be scared of them.

"Whatever, Heath, stop messing around. You can't even tell that's human," she muttered. Spear came ambling back in with True's pack in his arms.

Seizing the distraction, Otsana grabbed the pack. She met their glare for a second, then dumped it out with a rough shake. All their things clattered on the dusty tile. Loot and food and personal items.

They were going to *kill* her.

"Killjoy," Doorslammer said, tilting True's head with a pull of their hair. Appraising and displaying. A new slimy gleam in his eye made True's skin crawl. True's stomach churned. They shifted, feigning discomfort to test the bindings.

The gun hit the floor with a heavy thud. The other two factioneers paused to watch Otsana heft it. Fiddle with the mechanisms until the magazine popped. Raised an eyebrow at the bullets.

A sharp gasp and the echo of skin hitting skin sparked the air.

"Bugger bit me," Spear hissed.

"What, are you scared?" Otsana clicked the magazine back in. Then, horrifyingly, aimed at Radio. True's heart skipped the next few beats. She wouldn't. At night? The noise would echo for miles.

She clicked the safety off. Okay, time to leave. True did the first thing that popped into their brain and opened their mouth. "Where did Tweedledum go? Did you fuck up that bad? They had to run off without you?"

Her face bunched, she was too easy to goad.

Molten pain burst at the corner of True's eye. Blood trickled from the fresh injury. Red stained their image of Otsana receding, blood marking the handle of the gun.

"I'm right, huh?" They tracked the passing of the gun from Otsana to Doorslammer.

The temperature in that kitchen must have gone up two or three degrees, by the way sweat beaded on their skin. That fresh injury throbbed with heat. Otsana returned armed with a damp white square in place of the gun. Alcohol cut the smoke stench as she scrubbed the tiny volcano on their temple.

"Get off me." They contorted, but there wasn't exactly a lot of room to flee. She flicked their forehead, held up a hollow plastic needle filled with glossy red blood.

"Hrōkr went ahead to the next After Market," she said, taunting them with the tiny vial of their blood. "And all you can do about it is sit there and stew."

"Should you be telling them that?" Spear finally found his voice again. Otsana rolled her eyes, scraping True up and down like she had at the market. Her brown eyes held so much cold they swore they felt the chill.

"Like I said, not even human," she said. Then she was gone, waving the tiny vial in Radio's direction. "What about that one?"

Spear shook his head, "there's something wrong inside that head."

The conversation moved out of sight.

"Alright, well, drain them, too."

"Now?" Doorslammer chimed in.

"Yes! Then we can haul twenty bags of spoiled blood across to provinces!" Otsana said with a heavy coat of sarcasm. Her voice came from farther now, a different room. Doorslammer straightened his collar with an attitude.

"She thinks she's such hot shit," he grumbled under his breath, his halitosis rolled over True's bruised cheek. He was staring again. True ground their jaw against the panic swelling under their skin. They thought when he lifted his hand it was to push their hair from their ugly face to ogle it.

He stuck his sweaty, sooty, sausage dinger inside their scar.

What the *fuck*.

True ripped their whole body back. Bile rose to the back of their tongue, and panic, and they threw themself against the zip-ties as much to perish the sensation before it clawed itself into their brain as to get away from him. The chair flailed on one spindly leg, tilting like a defunct carnival ride.

"Cut it out. Hey!" Doorslammer punted the chair. True landed on their arm, felt a pop, swore. "Shut up."

They braced for the next blow. The heel sank into their gut and they groaned through gritted teeth.

"You really are feral," he said, and toed the canyon of their scar. "Gross."

Then the weight vanished. He shoved the gun into his waistband and he was gone. And True stayed very, very quiet.

And they kept quiet until the first pinking of the sky through the window over the sink. Spear had taken over guard while it had been dead dark, and he'd been squirming for the better part of that time. Any minute now. True spied from barely cracked eyes. Sheer willpower kept their breathing steady in spite of the anticipation leaking through their shot nerves.

Any minute now.

If their heart beat much harder it was bound to pop. The factioneer cleared his throat, plucked at the waistband of his pants as if that would alleviate the pressure on his bladder. He threw a glance at the captives, bound to chairs and sleeping. Then, finally, turned and hurried out the back door.

Slowly—but not too slowly, the guard would only be gone a few minutes at most. They were banking a lot on how full his bladder was—they heaved onto their knees, ass in the air with the chair sat like a turtle shell on top of them. They tested the wood arm they'd landed on and sure enough, it gave. Ha, that dumbass, Heath or whatever, had cost himself a prisoner.

They wiggled the arm, wincing at the crackling wood. It took several long seconds to free the arm from the rest of the chair. Freedom, at last. They extricated their other arm and lowered the chair to the tile.

They crammed all their stuff haphazardly into their pack. Everything had been left where Otsana dumped it, except the gun.

Speaking of which, they eased themself across the sooty tile. Doorslammer draped on the living room couch, mouth hung open. Crouching next to him, they watched his eyes flicked under his eyelids. It would be so, so easy to kill him. Easy, but too time-consuming.

They eased the gun from his belt. Snuck to the kitchen window opposite the back door. Their hand pressed to the cool pane when they hesitated. Every beat of their heart careened them closer to Spear marching back in and turned this silent escape into a brawl that they weren't in any condition to fight. And yet. They huffed, retreating from the window.

As much as they hated Radio, and aside from the fact it had brought this on itself by not taking one or two dozen hints, True wasn't so dead inside that they would abandon it to these vampires. Besides, it had *tried* to help them.

The factioneers had fastened a belt too-tight around its head and in its mouth. Its cheek squished out the top and bottom and drool dribbling past crooked bottom teeth. Leaving it would have been such an easy solution though. They pinched Radio's nose shut.

It blinked awake much more placidly than True would have. They pressed a finger to their lips for good measure before making quick work of the zip-ties. For once they were grateful for its preternatural silence.

They slipped out the window, landing on the balls of their feet. By the time they cast back, Radio had vanished. Never mind, they took back that bit about liking its quiet.

They forced themself to walk and not run across the lawn. No such thundering from their heavy boots or tripping on an abandoned hose was costing them this escape. They reached the ditch before the freeway and stopped to orient themself the right way. They had to get to the next After Market before the Red Faction blew it up.

A gentle morning breeze dried their tongue and they reached for the bandana around their neck. It wasn't there. Lost and forgotten in the chaos of escaping. Damn it. They couldn't help the twinge of regret that briefly tightened their throat. Never mind it. They shrugged their pack in place. People would just have to deal with seeing their scar until they found a new bandana.

A light tap on the back of their hand startled them half out of their skin.

"Damn, Radio," they huffed. Of course it was still here, it had the self-preservation of a panda cub. It held out a familiar blue square of cloth. Deep red filled each hairline groove in the skin of its hands. They snatched the bandana from it.

"...Thank you," they said, reluctantly, after the bandana was secure around their face. "Now shove off."

Radio shuffled from foot to foot, hands lost in the loose fabric of its raggedy beaded poncho so it looked like a cartoon sheet ghost that had sprouted human legs. Wet dripped from its black clothes. True stared hard at its steady, puffy eyes. At the red on its swollen, bruised mouth.

It took a hesitant step back. They motioned for it to keep going. This was it, no more playing Post-Apocalyptic Daycare. They didn't need a follower fish. Radio took another hesitant step, straight into the shallow dip of the ditch. It fell in slow motion, and gasped—the loudest sound True had ever heard come out of its mouth—when it landed in the cold run-off. The splash made True flinch. They shot a cursory glance at the farmhouse and swore under their breath. There was movement in the window.

The realization hadn't even fully set in when they bolted. Their boots hit the asphalt, they didn't spare a second glance back.

5
The City of Crows

The eroded framework of the next city appeared by midafternoon the next day. By then they'd picked up on the second set of footsteps hitting the pavement behind them and had pushed themself farther than they should have to try to shake it. No luck. And their breath was starting to taste like fresh blood.

They stopped to drink from their canteen and peel their sweat-soaked coat off, all while listening to their chaser get closer, falter, and finally stop. That was all the proof they needed to confirm their suspicions that it was Radio. Although the miles of following in complete silence had been pretty damning already. One of the farmhouse factioneers would have taken the opportunity to crack True over the head.

Whatever. They didn't have time to stop and shoo Radio off. Shrugging their pack into place, they set off at a brisk walk, headed west. The Red Faction could already be at the After Market, slinking around the hidden stalls, planting bombs in rusted eavestroughs. That thought alone squeezed a little extra speed out of their tired body.

What their plan was once they got there, they had no clue. Convincing a bunch of grouchy corpse robbers and merchants to uproot would be like walking barefoot on shattered glass.

Why kill the After Market? There had always been rumours that the Red Faction picked off scavengers. Shaken loners cropped up in the market streets on occasion, claiming they had been hauled off to Red Faction headquarters and escaped as a lone survivor of unspeakable horrors.

But it was one thing to kill a few scavengers and entirely another to destroy the After Market. It was the After Market that had pushed this stretch of world across the line from post-apocalypse and kept it there. Out of the starvation years and into survival. And even that had happened only recently. Nobody was ready for it to burn up yet. And nobody would believe the Red Faction was stupid enough to try.

They reached the outskirts of the city as the sun hit the spiky line of the horizon. Knee-high wild grass gave way to young trees and wildflowers that upheaved the sidewalks. Bushes spread unchecked up the sides of buildings that had once held offices and living spaces. A scavenger could spend months clearing some of those apartment complexes and hotels. Scorch marks and ash pits marked the street before the front doors of certain buildings to indicate to civilians and scavengers alike that those ones were a corpse-free place to rest.

In recent months, some of the less nomadically-inclined civilians had begun to make homes in the upper floors.

A rabbit skittered across their path, dodging from undergrowth to undergrowth. That would make good stew one day. The After Market would be yawning awake now, a tiny constellation of oily light reflected at the fresh night sky. True hurried through the abandoned streets. They had to hope the Market hadn't moved since the last time they were here. Then again, maybe that would be a good sign. Maybe somebody else had sniffed the Faction out.

No such luck. They ducked into the underground parking garage and saw the lights.

The Market popped its bones; merchants laying out wares on the threadbare cloths draped over makeshift tables; a cook near the entrance stoked a fire under a giant cauldron of perpetual stew that had been going approximately since the beginning of the apocalypse. The cook bid farewell to his latest patron with a cheery smile. A greasy rat tail fell between his bony shoulder blades and kept his greying hair out of his fine-lined face. His eyes were of the wide, slightly downturned variety that gave his expression a sort of lost-lamb-esque quality that some people might call inviting, but True would call eerie.

"Jonesy." True lifted their hand in greeting.

The cook nodded back, smile souring at the edges. "Little early, True, gotta give this new meat some time to marinate."

"Not here for food. I need you to keep people out of the Market." Even as they spoke, scavengers were trickling into the potential death trap. Jonesy's gaze lingered on the tender spot above True's eye. They weren't his favourite scavenger, not that they were anybody's favourite scavenger, but Jonesy had no use for those who didn't fall sway to his friendly chatter. And True had no use for his chatter, until now. People liked Jonesy, they would listen to him. Or at least he had favours he could cash in with pretty much everyone who passed. True would just have to buckle down and owe him for the rest of their miserable life.

"Hit your head a tad hard, huh?" he said.

"No, I'm serious."

"I think your lisp's worse today, maybe you should have a seat. I'll get you a bowl." He was already turning his back. True slammed their fists on the lip of the cauldron. Stew sloshed over the dirty ground.

"Galya's dead!" Their shout ricocheted off the cement rafters and bounced around between Jonesy's ears. They could practically hear it pinging off his synapses. At last, the cook did move. There was that prying glint in his eyes again that made True recoil, regret tying their tongue. They had needed him to care to listen, but saying her name felt like giving him too much.

He hooked a rickety three-legged stool closer to True, expression all wrinkled forehead and faint frown and open arms.

"Who is Galya?" he asked in a tone that was too soft and made their bullshit sensor tingle.

Whatever, they'd needed him to listen and now he was listening. They bit their tongue to loosen the tie.

"A merchant from the Market I watched get blown up. She's dead. Everybody died. And everyone here will die, too, if you don't quit dicking around and do what I told you."

Now Jonesy's arm was around their shoulders, making their skin crawl. They shrugged, earlobes all but scraping their shoulders to force him away, and he slid off, carrying on like he didn't notice they were half a step from jamming his own foot into his mouth.

"Sorry your friend died, I know how it is. But we're survivors, eh? You and I might not get along much but you keep on coming back and I'll always be around. You don't gotta worry about any explosions here."

Ugh, fine! He wasn't going to be any help. True scoffed and turned on their heels. If Jonesy wouldn't do anything, they'd find someone who would. Every second wasted was another person unwittingly wandering into a deathtrap.

A tall scavenger paused at Jonesy's beaten counter and slide something across to him.

"For the stew," a deep voice said. The trade disappeared into Jonesy's apron pocket. True was more interested in how clean the arm attached to the scavenger was.

The not-scavenger hesitated. A slight catch, mid-reach, the tilt of their head a few degrees and the flicker of lazy, venomous eyes sliding sideways to glimpse True in the periphery. The soot and blood from the first After Market had been scrubbed away, but their unsettlingly delicate features had been acid-etched into True's brain.

True prickled, on them in an instant, just in time for the factioneer to shove an empty backpack at True. The distraction bought the factioneer a second to bolt.

True batted away the pack and pelted after them.

A deep boom rattled the concrete, sending both runner and chaser sprawling. True landed on hands and knees and braced for the second explosion. The bigger one that would force hungry flames through the tight underground parking garage. Farther up the ramp, the factioneer jumped to their feet, leaving behind a gleeful cackle.

"Better run faster, scavenger!"

Their taunt slithered down to True's ears. The wails of the injured and confused rang through the air, dust floated up towards the entrance. A real scavenger, one True vaguely recognized, crept down the ramp not far from the space the factioneer had occupied moments earlier. Dust turned her narrow eyes watery, ringing them in red. She had one hand pressed to her ear, wincing, a pink wire tangled in her fingers. Her other hand gripped a dented metal bat like it was her lifeline.

"What ha—" she jolted like a code in her brain had misfired. Ragdolling down the ramp, the pink cable and the scuffed disc attached to it clacked to a stop just beyond her reach. It crunched into sharp plastic bits under a factioneer's hiking boot.

A surgical mask hid much of the factioneer's features, but the white streak over her brow and twined up into her hair ratted Otsana out. Her eyes rolled as she kicked the remnants of the cochlear implant, wiping her blade on her thigh. The tall factioneer broke the dust screen behind her, now also sporting a mask. They caught a lock of Otsana's hair and twirled it in a motion that True could have called grossly affectionate, if not for the blood slugging downhill towards them. *Affectionate* was a softer word than Otsana deserved.

"Convenient." Was all she got out before True launched themself at her. Backpedalling, she ducked out of the way of their shovel by a hair.

"Hrōkr," a guttural call left her throat. Her spectral factioneer friend materialized out of the dust to hook their improbably long arms around True's neck, noose tight. They draped themself over True's shoulder.

"Yes, my darling?" They purred in a voice so deep it was unsettling. "Do you know this little scavenger?"

"They gutted Heath."

"I did not." True said, invoking a hard squeeze from the anaconda around their neck. Their heartbeat became a thud-thud in the swelling veins under their skin. Damn their tongue.

"No more from you," the factioneer said, squeezing tighter. Instinct took over for a stupid panic-stricken instant. The shovel hit the ramp as they clawed at the too-tight beast arm.

"You are such a pain in my ass." Otsana drew a boxcutter from the confines of her sleeve. Hrōkr's grip loosened marginally, permitting True a gasp of dusty air. In spite of

Hrōkr's lankiness it felt like they could flex their bicep and pop True's head off.

True flailed and sank their teeth into Hrōkr's bare arm. Their sharp intake of breadth was music to True's ears. That brief, instinctual flinch gave them a smidge of space to drop to the pavement and grab their shovel.

Crack—on Hrōkr's leg. The giant went down on one knee.

Otsana barrelled True over between one breath and the next. Face full of concrete, teeth full of grit. She stuck her blade to the pulse in their neck and pressed. Then, vanished.

They scrambled to their feet, wheeling about to face the scene unfolding before them. Otsana on the ground. Feral clump of black rags thumping her head onto the concrete with alarming viciousness. Hrōkr stretching a long arm to catch the rags.

True hefted their shovel and swung the edge into Hrōkr's elbow. Bone cracked, Hrōkr dropped Radio. Its feet hit the concrete and it rocked back, driving its elbow into Hrōkr's gut. They absorbed the blow but stumbled, only to lose their footing on the blood-slicked ramp. True swiped at their head. Too slow.

Hrōkr flung concrete dust straight into True's face. They staggered back, choking on the fragments, eyes stinging. They blinked tears from their eyes in time to see Hrōkr hoist Otsana's limp body over their shoulder. Against their better judgement, True let them retreat.

True wiped the blood from their neck, regarding Radio while they caught their breath.

"You're kinda scary, ya know?"

A new wail started up nearby, silhouettes gathered at the mouth of the ramp. Either shadow dwellers or more factioneers. They would have to find a different way out. True allowed themself an extra beat to double-check that all the straps on their pack were secure, then dove into the chaos.

Sweat stung in the open wounds they'd collect. Half the air they pulled into their heaving lungs was concrete dust. They swung their shovel again, again, again, again. More often than not they struck at ghosts. The factioneers and dwellers crept through the dark and the dust with the efficiency of sharks prowling familiar waters. True hopped fallen scavengers in pursuit of mirages, the exits ever-moving out of reach.

Swing. Swing. Swing-thump. Swing.

Their arms grew leaden. They were in good shape, but they weren't Heracles. They tripped over the body of a merchant whose face had been slashed so that True only recognized her from her fin-shaped hand. An agonized shriek echoed off the damage concrete supports. Ahead, the ferrety shape of Jonesy straddled a body, wielding a butcher knife the length of his forearm. His soppy eyes darted from True to a third person who emerged from the swirling dust between them. A bold red cross shone alarm-light bright on the stranger's back. True rammed their shovel handle into the base of the factioneer's skull. The factioneer's head whipped and True hauled her back to acquaint her eye socket with their fist. Their knuckles popped, the factioneer staggered, and they kicked her into the dust with a heel to the soft flesh below her sternum.

"Help us get out of here," Jonesy cried from his place on the floor, a young merchant cradled close to his chest. Thick grey dust turned the merchant two-d and stickeresque, natural skin tone and depth stamped flat except for a fat ribbon of blood running from a swollen round welt on her crown. That wound looked nasty. It looked like the kind of wound that would give her trouble walking.

"Fuck off," True exhaled, unconvincingly since they had to lean over and rest their hands on their knees. They needed a minute. It was broiling hot down in that car garage and their throat felt like someone had shot a sandblaster into their open mouth.

"I can't carry her on my own," Jonesy's plaintive whine was punctuated by the merchant woman's groan. Consequences of Jonesy trying to heave her up. Her ankle had been lost under a chunk of rubble and her leg stretched out uselessly from her otherwise unbloodied body. She would have a better shot left there were the rubble hid her from the incoming shadow dwellers. "True—!"

"Fine! Fine, be quiet," True hissed, cutting across to Jonesy and the merchant. He had his arms around her, coddling her head. If nothing else, Jonesy had lived as a satellite colony of this After Market for as long as True had been visiting, and he knew his way around. True was pretty sure they'd been going in circles on their own. Plus, in spite of the misguided effort, True chewed on the nothing that maybe Jonesy meant some of that plastered-on honey-thick caring.

They wedged between his arms to clamp her mouth shut and kicked the rubble off. Spit and hot breath slapped their palm, chased by a couple warm tears. They hooked the merchant under her armpits.

"To the exit," they instructed.

They wound through the dungeon, skirting silhouettes, hopping lumps. The merchant woman sagged off their left side. They were right about the welt, she wobbled uncontrollably, stopping twice to empty her stomach while just ahead Jonesy took his sweet time leading them to safety. Consciousness kited around her. There, but useless as far as running went.

At last, they came to a short, narrow hall that ended in a metal door. Giant curls of paint shed from its surface and lay in the dirt piled before it. A flit of black in the haze caught True's eye as they approached the edge of the hall.

"Radio!" they called just once before ducking into the hall. If it heard, it heard.

They emerged on the other side of the door to clearer air and a night sky. Escape led them deeper into the city, where all that remained of the chaos was a shrill ringing in their ears. Well, that, and the sickness in their gut. They had made it just in time to witness the downfall of another After Market.

Darkness shrouded the city, air chummed with the bitter aftertaste of iron and pyrotechnics. Shadows shifted and grimy windows betrayed glimpses of motion. Reflected, or revealed?

Which side were the dwellers standing on? Chilly fingers traced True's sweat-soaked back.

"Where's your stay?" they asked.

"We just left it."

Great.

They needed to get low, fast. Get off the street. Shut up, preferably in a windowless room with a deadbolt. Unfortunately, they were glued to a shivering, sweat-sticky merchant whose foot looked more mottled and bulgy in every patch of moonlight they crossed. They made poor time hobbling through the dark streets. Desperation rolled off them, a siren's call enticing shadow dwellers to veer off from the death beacon that was the late After Market. True could feel hungry stares tracking them as they swept every crevice and doorframe for a place to shove themself and their limpets.

A shape darted from the street corner, all amorphous in black rags. Jonesy squeaked—could he be any more rat-like?— knife glinting. Idiots. True slammed their shovel up in the nick of time to pin Jonesy's knife arm. The metal lion's head on the butt sparked off the brick wall with a wince-worthy clang and a curse from Jonesy. The would-be shadow dweller wavered short of arms-reach, a thin red line opened on the soft tissues beneath its eye.

"What the hell is wrong with you?" Jonesy shoved True off.

"You," True replied.

They levelled the tip of their shovel at Radio, aimed at the fresh blood. "That counted, we're even." And then, in case it took that as an invitation to join this little clusterfuck they were trying to dump, they added, "fuck outta here."

As if to underline their warning, the merchant moaned, the noise sandwiched between panic and pain. Radio studied her, too-dark eyes flicking from the merchant to Jonesy's knife. It rocked back on its heels and True poked their shovel into its papercut, forcing a wider distance.

"Follow me and I'll put my knife in your eye," they said, pushing past it. They didn't have a knife. They had a shovel, and a gun. Fucking whatever. By the time they'd reached the end of the street, Radio had dissolved into the dark.

Rubber soles scraped on asphalt. The merchant woman yelped, her weight veering True off-balance. The dweller matched her pitch with a screech, they set upon her. Mid-strike her flailing hand hit solid flesh. Fingers disappeared into a rotted mouth. The crunch of broccoli, the snap of green twigs. Her unholy ear-splitting wail did nothing to drown out the *snap-crunch* of the merchant's fingers breaking. Seconded only by the nauseating tearing of flesh when the dweller shook its head.

Forcing down bile, True jammed their shovel between the undulating mass of dweller and merchant. A wet crackle-pop cut the merchant's cries to a gurgle. The dweller reared back, stringy flesh flinging from its mouth. Gnashing, the dweller lunged teeth-first a True. Bloodshot eyes rolling, a ragged bit of skin stuck between its molars. Its rank breath brough the bile straight back.

Blood pooled beneath them, turning the sidewalk slick. They cracked the shovel handle up into the dweller's jaw. That brough them an inch of space. Which they lost, instantly, to a slip. Hot blood splashed onto their shaking muscles as they hit the concrete hard. The dweller shoved into their personal space. Writhing, sucking air into stalled lungs, they struck out and by sheer luck knocked the dweller.

Where the fuck was Jonesy?

There, loitering at the edge of the tussle. Being useless.

"Jonesy! Knife!" True gasped, trying to snap the cook to action. No luck. They smacked the dweller once more, reached and tore Jonesy's knife from his slimy clutches. The dweller seized their shovel. It hit the brick a few feet away. The dweller dove. True braced. The blade skimmed the dweller's teeth. A sharp thunk, a thud, the knife punched a bruise onto True's sternum and blood showered them. The dweller was dead before its head bounced off the ground, a butcher knife jutting from its open mouth.

The night seethed, predators raced toward the fresh kills, and True allowed themself exactly three seconds to catch their breath. Three seconds to stare at the dried blood on the lion's head. They glanced down, just once, just on a whim, at the bruise on the dead merchant's head.

"Why didn't you do anything?" they asked.

Jonesy was quick with a stammer and a voice notched up two notes. "I don't know, I just—it all happened and—"

"And you wanted her dead before she could tattle on you?" They turned the lion-shaped bruise toward him. He probably should have just stabbed her, but then how would she have lived long enough for him to use her to manipulate True? Jonesy scrambled for an excuse.

"It was an accident."

True quit listening halfway into the lie. They had half a mind to cram their shovel up his squirrelly broken nose, but it had landed out of reach. Wrenching the knife free, they whipped it at him before either of them really had a chance to catch the decision. With a cry, Jonesy crumpled over his leg. The knife skittered off behind him.

The wound would be shallow, True was sure. They didn't have the strength left for a decent blow, no matter how wicked sharp the blade. But it would hurt, and it would fester, and Jonesy was going to deal with that all on his own.

"Oops," they said, and turned their back on him.

"Wait," Jonesy groaned, "wait, you can't leave me."

And yet, they were leaving. They stooped to grab their shovel. Jonesy rambled at their backside.

"It was survival, True, you would have done the same, you hypocrite."

That did it. Against their better judgement, which seemed par for the course these days, they stalked back to him. He'd gotten his hands on the knife. They batted it out of their way, grabbed him by the collar and got real close to his mean, bloodied face.

"You better keep out of my way, because if I ever see you again, *I* will bite *your* finger off," they spit, and for good measure they drove their knee into his nice new gash. He dropped, crying in agony, and they left him there.

Let him snake his way through a night in the city without the safety of the merchants he had backstabbed. He had his knife, and he certainly knew how to use it.

Survival, indeed.

6
The Lonely Highway

Morning again. They walked the shoulder of the freeway outside the city. Pride and stubbornness kept their feet from dragging, but they were tired. Bone heavy. Heart worn. They didn't know where to go from here.

The sky was lightening to a frail eggshell blue and a gentle breeze soothed their burning lungs. They stopped. Didn't sit, just stopped walking, and waited, and watched the sky morph from robin's egg to cornflower.

Eventually, almost predictably, a familiar small black lump materialized at their side.

"Not in the mood," True grumbled. Radio remained, not making noise, but not leaving either.

"Go away."

It shuffled just outside their periphery. As if it believed in extreme out of sight, out of mind. This was not the morning for its shenanigans. True rounded on it, fists clenched so hard their nails bit through the old gauze on their palms.

"Quit following me, you creepy little thhhi—sth—thss—" they cut off with a frustrated shout. Radio watched, wide-eyed. It held one of its arms close to its torso, the other it lifted in a half-hearted shield. But that was all.

"I don't know what you want but I don't have it. I will never have it, and even if I did I would never give it to you. Forget about whatever made you think following me was a good idea and fuck. Off." They punctuated their laugh words with two sharp shoves to Radio's chest, forcing it back. This time was final. Radio was going to walk the fuck away and True was going to watch it leave until they were sure it would never come back.

Except instead of walking away, Radio pressed a single finger to the bridge of its nose and drew it down, tracing a mirror image of True's scar.

True's anger burst; a wildfire; a spark to gunpowder.

Radio shifted deftly to the side of their punch. Catching them by the elbow, it held firm, trapping them in close proximity. Only for a second, then it dropped them and opened its mouth. It took a beat for True to comprehend what they were looking at. They had never seen the remnants of a cut-out tongue before.

Judging by the way the two sides buckled over each other, it had been a savage hack job. Nothing like a reminder of human suffering to douse a rage fire. True's fist unfolded, momentum lost.

"No wonder you never talk." Dick thing to say. True cringed internally. Radio grinned, closing its teeth on the ugly scene. It didn't seem particularly bothered. Sighing, True scuffed their sole on the pavement and noticed for the first tie the puddle of blood growing there.

A fat droplet fell from Radio's other, immobile arm and plipped on the dirt. It had been injured. Probably in that tussle with Otsana. Images of the boxcutter she'd held to their throat conjured in their mind.

Unclipping their pack, they gestured to Radio's injured arm.

"Let me look at that," they said as they rummaged for their first aid kit. Salve, check. They scooped some out. But the last of their bandages were in tatters around their hands. Damn, right. Their bandana would work, but... well, actually, it was their only usable option.

Reluctantly, they unfastened the bandana from around their face and took careful hold of Radio's arm. Its skin was mottled, and not only by blood. The dark olive tint of its skin was lost somewhere under a mass of pink and bloodless white. Frowning, True pushed its loose sleeve up to its elbow and uncovered more scar than skin. Burn marks twisted like ropes up its arm and further into the places hidden by its clothes. It shivered and tugged its sleeve down again, covering the scars.

"Sorry," the word came unbidden and unfamiliar to True's lips, they trailed off, uncertain how to finish that sentence, and settled for tying the bandana tight over the fresher wound instead. They fumbled the knot a couple times, fingers sluggish and a little alien. When sharks stopped moving, they died. When True stopped moving, exhaustion caught up.

They had to keep going to the next After Market, and maybe the next one after that. Or the Market after the one after that. Until they got there in time, convinced the right people. Then...

then what? One Market survived while the Red Faction crushed ten? True bit the side of their tongue until they tasted blood, and lingered a beat longer with the only other person on the entire planet who knew what was going on.

There was one tiny upside to having a stalker: It sort of made the end of the end of the world a smidge less lonely.

"I don't know what to do," they sighed. Then turned around and kept walking, their soles scuffing on the blacktop.

7
The Farmer on the Road

Fresh air hushing through the untrimmed wild grass could coax ideas out of the deep dark wrinkles of the brain. Sunlight, even pale and wan, warmed their skin and all the thready vessels below. Nothing like a soothing stroll to keep the body in motion and relax the mind.

That was, when every inch of said body didn't ache. When said brain had been allotted more than five minutes of sleep. When the damned grass wasn't making them sneeze every second of the day. True stomped their way through the one hundredth sneezing fit, each stomp heavier than the last, as if they could crush the sneezes under their heel. It was childish. They were fine with that.

Radio padded quietly along behind them in high-laced hiking shoes that should have made a lot more noise than it did. Miserable creature.

They kicked a rock and listened to the crack of it against a distant tree trunk with an inkling of satisfaction. Focus, they had to focus. If the other scavengers were going to be yellow bellies about the Red Faction—and after Jonesy, True decided they would be—they needed a new plan.

All the ideas they drummed up ended in personal disaster. Death, death, and death with a side of fighting. What a fun variety of options.

They slowed to a stop, squinting at the sunbaked asphalt. One goal stood as the foundation for all their plots: Galya had traded her gun for revenge, and they were damn well going to honour that trade.

"Anything interesting down there?" A deep voice startled True, they flinched about six inches into the air and hard left of their skeletal system.

"Motherfuck!" they swore when their lungs relocated inside their ribcage.

"Caught you sleeping, did I?" The culprit, a suntanned behemoth farmer, chuckled. True didn't share his amusement, instead eyeing the three other forms that lurked along the edge of the copse that had hidden their approach. Four to one, those were bad odds.

"You look rough, bud, got into a tussle, huh?" The farmboy, who was batting three for three on opening his mouth to ask a question, stared openly south of True's eyes. Grimacing, true turned their bad side away from him.

"The After Market was attacked," the said.

Farmboy hemmed and hawed and nodded for an eternity, rocking his whole body with the waggles of his head. While he digested, the smallest of the forms flitted off along the edge of the ditch. Farmboy's head bobbled toward the movement, his gargantuan hand drifting to his hip, only stalled by a motion from on of his remaining buddies.

Right, that was as good a sign as any to leave.

Then Farmboy opened his mouth. "What's your name there, bud?"

True bit their tongue to keep from snapping, only because they had just enough active brain cells to know they'd lose that fight.

"True... Gallows."

Laughter brightened Farmboy. He was, evidently, the kind of person who laughed with his whole body.

"There's a name!"

They ground down until they tasted blood. At least he hadn't ended on a question mark this time.

"I'm Linc." He stuck out his bear paw to shake. True accepted it. "This is Mu and Cal."

The two remaining lingerers had made it to the crumbling shoulder of the highway, much to close for comfort. One tall, olive-skinned, with a face like a barn owl. Ther other shorter, with crossed arms and grey eyes that tracked everything. As long as they were comparing people to animals, that one looked like a feral cat. Each had a pack.

The tallest, the one Linc called Mu, rivaled Farmboy in size, but there was something infinitely less threatening about him. Maybe it was the way he waved until Cal elbowed his hip.

"And the other one?" True asked. They didn't care what any of these strangers names were, but they wanted Farmboy to know that they knew about the fourth person lurking around.

"That'd be Eliza. You don't gotta worry yourself about her." Linc said.

Like hell they didn't.

"Why don't you join us for supper? It's about that time and you can tell me about the Market," Farmboy clapped their shoulder, and seemed to take pleasure in the way True's teeth clattered.

True had hoped that part had whistled through the space between his ears and floated harmlessly into the atmosphere. The sun sank lower on the horizon and cast long burgundy shadows on the Earth. It was about time to start hunting for shelter, not sit down for a meal and a chat. Then again, safety came with numbers.

"You got a stay nearby?" They asked. If Farmboy Linc came equipped with a farmhouse, they wouldn't despise one miserable evening at his fire. A neon smile sparked on his mug. True doubted there was such a thing as a question that didn't make him beam like a kindergarten teacher. It was deeply unsettling in that it gave them the nagging feeling that they were the kindergartener.

"Sure!" he said. He strolled to the middle of the road and dragged his heel across it in a large, sloppy X. "Here looks good. Not too far a walk for you, is it?"

True blinked at the imaginary X for a long minute, waiting for Linc to crack another smile and drop the joke. But the only thing he dropped was his pack onto the asphalt.

How was this guy real?

"Yeah, no." If they walked really improbably fast they would make it to a ghost town that should have been somewhere along this highway. They'd expected to come across it already but apparently they were dragging their feet more than they thought.

"Aw, don't tell me you're afraid of a few shadow crawlies."

"Not afraid," True said. "Not inviting them to munch on me either."

A baseball mitt of a hand engulfed their shoulder, squeezing them tight to Farmboy Linc's sweaty side. His giant arm stretched around True and their pack with ease. Sweeping wide, he encompassed the road and his lingerers in his reach. "That's what our little buddies are for. No shadow crawly gets the jump on a well-trained bodyguard, and mine have to be well-trained because I got a lot of body to guard!"

Mu's towering shape had materialized over at the edge of the copse, and he lumbered back towards the X on the road with a fallen tree slung over his shoulder. Two packs slumped beside the X, but instead of kneeling beside the packs or pawing through the underbrush where True expected to see him, Cal strode down the blacktop. Back the way True had come from, the direction the third lingerer had disappeared towards. Linc bent, so close they could hear the wet pulling-apart of his lips and teeth and tongue while they watched a furious ball of limbs and rags erupt from the long grass and tumble on the asphalt.

Damn it. It wasn't like True cared much whether Radio lived or got torn apart by the road bandits, but at least it had a history of interfering in their favour.

"And if they fail they get eaten first, gives us plenty of time to run," he whispered in their ear. The ball splintered into two clumps, the clump that was Radio leaping its feet only to be seized by the Cal.

Linc guffawed, obnoxiously loud.

Yeah, there was a word. Guffaw. Farmboy Linc guffawed like he wanted every shadow dweller in a mile radius to come test his bodyguards.

Maybe they'd join the Red Faction instead. The Faction was a group of slimy brainless salamanders but at least they had the conviction to look the world in the eye while they lit it on fire. And True had never witnessed a factioneer tossing another factioneer to the cannibals.

Cold metal dug into True's cheek, chilling them from scalp to sole. The hammer of the handgun clicked in place. "You don't like my jokes? Well maybe I should kill you right now and feed you to that shadow crawly, huh?"

"If you kill me," True said, slow, reaching for the right words through the exhaustion haze and adrenaline spike, "you'll never know what happened to the After Market."

"I'll find another survivor."

"There aren't any."

Linc's grip tightened, turning True's breaths shallow. He could probably squeeze them until they popped, never mind that gun.

"How'd you make it out?"

"I knew it was coming."

Click.

They flinched. Pain, then darkness. That's how it went, right? If you were lucky. Just like a concussion, except you didn't wake up afterward with a splitting headache.

It came as a pleasant surprise when True opened their eyes and found the only ringing in their ear was Linc bent over in uproarious laughter. Face red, whole body heaving. Well, not pleasant. But a surprise, nonetheless.

"That's not fucking funny." They shoved him, causing barely a hiccup in his guffawing.

"Sure it is." He jostled them and held out his gun, trigger finger wiggling as if to say *look, stupid, I was never near that trigger.* But True had heard the hammer on that tiny silver thing strike. The echo of their own doom wasn't going to fall out of their skull just because Linc brayed louder than a donkey. That jackass *had* pulled the trigger.

"Tell you what though, this thing is small, but it keeps those guys in line." Another laugh at his ingenuity. Another bone-jostling pat on True's back. "Come on, sit at my fire tonight. Tell me about the Market, and I'll provide the food. I'm starving."

True hesitated, gathering their wits. Food was food, and the sky had darkened in the time they'd lost to Farmboy Linc's shenanigans. Glancing up the road to where Radio had been penned-in by the feral cat and his fox twin, they gave in to following Linc. A night out in the open it was. They'd sleep with one eye open, if they slept at all.

Flint sparked, fire blazed. All five travelers curled into the safety within the light's boundaries. No matter how well-armed or well-guarded a person made themselves, the dark was the dark. Even the night sky needed the moon to keep it safe.

By the time Linc had knifed open the tops of a few dented cans, True had fished a silver spoon from their loot bag. It had been hanging on someone's kokum's wall for so long that when they'd pried it off the paint beneath it had been shades lighter. Linc admired the red barn painted on the tip of the handle before swapping the spoon for a can of maple beans in True's hand.

Cat and Fox shoved Radio, hands bound, to its knees in the circle. What were their names again? Cal and Eliza? Yeah. Cal reached to accept a can from Linc, Eliza did not. Up close the fox looked effeminate, in a malnourished, vampiric kind of way. Unease had True looking twice at her sallow skin and sunken cheeks. Were her irises jiggling or was that a trick of the wavering flames?

"You're extra spooky in the dark, you know?" Linc interrupted their staring spree. He waved an open can at them. "The fire makes your face holes look all lit up like a jack o'lantern."

They leaned farther from the light of the flames. They wished he would pick a different reaction to their face. Preferably unnerved silence, which Cal seemed to have settled on. Or even the bald-faced staredown that Mu was giving them. At least Mu was doing it quietly.

"Hey, now, don't get all hurt on me, Trudy. Your skin's thicker than that, isn't it?" Linc was saying around a mouthful. It took True a beat to realize he was addressing them.

"It's True," they said.

"It is!"

Comedic gold. What a hilarious joke. True shoved a sporkful of beans in their mouth and waited for Farmboy Jokes to recover from his own comedy. At the peak of his hearty chucklefest, when his eyes were turned to slits by the breadth of his mouth, Mu stretched a long arm out and pressed his palm to the Eliza's. A kernel of corn slipped out between her knuckles but by the time it plipped on the ground the rest of the corn had disappeared past her gullet. She crammed the heal of her hand to her lips to smother the lurch from inhaling the food too fast.

Cal's knee tapped Mu's, stalling his next handful. True caught Cal's wary gaze boring into them while the laughter began to peter out and Mu retracted.

Shifting grass all along the highway harmonized with the popping coals to fill the precious quiet. Linc began to inflate. Barrel chest expanding in preparation for his next amazing quip or his one hundred millionth question.

"The Red Faction blew up two After Markets this week," True said. They truly could not stand another word out of his mouth, and the only peaceful option was to fill the silence with their own voice. Talking filled a few minutes, sneezing filled almost as many, and by the time they'd recovered, Linc had been thumping their back and chortling at them for just as long.

"Quite a kerfuffle you've got there," he butted his two cents in on the tailwinds of his laughter, affording True no space to reclaim the conversation. "You're headed to Vancouver then, huh? Far walk."

"Vancouver," True repeated, slowly. They'd been headed west, they knew the Faction had been encroaching into the middle provinces from that coast, but this was the first certain name they'd been given.

"Well, that's—hold on—Eliza!" he bellowed the last part. True winced, casting leery glances at the shadowed ditches. Fortunately, the only malinger was Radio, crouched on the shoulder just outside the circle of light. "The Red Faction works out of Vancouver, doesn't it?"

The fox woman lifted a vacant stare to Linc. Through Linc.

"Vancouver," she confirmed.

"Good girl."

As soon as his eyes were off her, the vacuous neutral expression waxed over Eliza's face hardened. Disgust, hate, hunger. Carved into the deep grooves of a predator's snarl. A chill settled in True's gut.

And Linc was too busy blabbing about her to even notice. "We picked her up in that city, she knows the area darn well, I'd say. She could probably lead you straight to the Faction headquarters, but I'm afraid I can't lend her out."

"You didn't give her any food," True said, the weight of the can in their hands set them on edge. They'd traded that spoon in good faith. Pawning off someone else's food wasn't fair trade, it was sleazy double-dealing, and liable to get both parties stabbed.

"Oh, don't go getting offended on me." Linc flapped his hand, his expression soured but didn't lose all the steeped-in amusement. He leaned towards them conspiratorially. Stage whispered. "Eliza's our very own shadow crawly, she's got a meal right there." He motioned to Radio.

A shadow dweller?

"A *meal?*" They clacked their teeth down on their tongue before they announced their whereabouts to any other shadow dwellers. But now Linc had finally let a frown settle on that wide jowl of his.

"I'd've thought you'd be more grateful, seeing as we've stopped this shadow crawly from making a meal of you!" Again, that motion to the lump of Radio on the road.

"Radio's not a shadow whatever," True said.

Farmboy cocked an eyebrow, his eyebrows were just barely plural. Much like his brain cells. He lingered on Radio for a long beat, holding his tongue for possibly the first time in his entire life. Another beat, and True began to wonder—hope—if he'd burst an aneurysm right there.

Unfortunately, he moved, words once again bubbling to the infinite fountain of his lips.

"Sure looks like a crawly."

True grunted in response. No matter how on edge Farmboy Linc and the three stooges put them, their body worked against them. Shutting down. Everything smudged around the edges. They were falling out of time with the resonance of the rest of the world.

Whatever Linc said next slid off their brain. Blink hard. They pinched themself. Why was the fox woman taking off her shirt?

No, thank goodness, she stopped with the hem bunched up at her ribs. Firelight reflected off a ragged purple scar that hooked from the bottom of her sternum to her hip. She waved her fingertips down the length of the scar as if presenting it to the crowd.

"To become part of the collective, you must feed the collective." Her fingers fanned from the scar to Radio, who sat like a disused puppet, swaying ever so slightly on moldering strings. "No missing body parts? Not one of us."

"Well go on then, prove it," Linc said.

"Don't be dumb," True cut in. Whoops, they hadn't thought that through, but all eyes were on them now. "Everybody out here is missing a body part." The hiss of their lisp clinging to each s drove their point home. Missing tooth, missing chunk of lip, missing strip of nose. None of which could be mistaken as a sacrifice to 'feed the collective'. There wasn't the meat for it there, for one.

Linc raised his hands, and for a brief instant True, addled, believed it was in mock surrender. But heaven forbid he use an ounce of sense. Instead, he wiggled his fingers.

"All ten fingers, all ten toes."

Well that just felt mean.

At a wave from Linc, the Eliza pushed her outstretched fingers into Radio's bubble, aiming for its face. At last, Radio moved, fast. Rope shreds fell from its wrists. A knife flashed in its fist. It grabbed her and yanked, and with a sharp cry she staggered back, her arm flopping free of its socket. Cal stepped into her place, already swinging. Radio dodged by a sliver, its hand darting to lock around the cat's arm. It turned his own momentum against him, dragging him past the trajectory of his swing into the hard point of its elbow. The impact echoed.

It occurred to True that radio had been *very* restrained with them. That it was hold back now, too, its knife angled away from Cal.

Lost in the dance of the fight, True missed Linc lumbering to his feet.

Dark metal flinted. The gun. He ate the space separating him from the fight in one stride. Metal met flesh, the hammer clicked a warning that froze Radio in place. By the end of a breath, the Cal had stumbled out of reach, leaking blood onto the warm asphalt, and Linc had manhandled Radio about so the gun pressed to its forehead.

"I told you, prove it." He gripped its jaw, his hand swallowing its chin. Malignancy had bubbled to the surface of his humour. Backlit by the fire, his grin looked more like bared teeth. Radio's knife twitched. He squeezed, distorting the shape of its face. Little bulges of bloodless skin and cheek muscle pushed between his knuckles. With a shake, he rattled its whole body. The knife clattered on the ground.

"You're a damn good fighter, but I'm in charge here. Me. And if I have to strip those ugly ass rags off your scrawny body to get an answer I will. I don't want to. But I will get my answer."

Radio was still still still. Black eyes wide and thin mouth pressed into a grim line. Linc drew back his gun as if to strike.

Froze.

True pressed the muzzle of their gun harder to the sunburned skin of his neck.

"Mine's loaded," they said.

One of those obnoxious jaw-splitting grins spread across Farmboy's thick mug. This was a joke to him. A joke he was in on. *Ha-ha, True, using my own dirty trick on me.* They could practically see the mirth glittering in his eyes.

Bang!

Recoil sizzled up their arm, shoving it off course. Now they were the puppet, and their strings jerked. Farmboy swore, a single fuck with his whole gut. Swiped at True. They had the presence to sidestep and level the gun at him again. An angry red burn marked a path under his eye where the bullet had skimmed too close. Thin, clear fluid drooled from the patch. In truth, they hadn't meant to hit him at all. But whatever worked.

"Seems I misjudged you." There was no laughter in him. He glared down at True, but they knew he couldn't see them. Not the purple smudged under their eyes, not the waver in their stance, not the tired sag of their shoulders. He wasn't that sharp, and all they were to him was an indescribably ugly face and a pair of ears to hear his great jokes.

Not that they were anything else to anyone else. It was just especially annoying coming from Linc.

"Gonna shoot me again, Trudy? Gonna leave my poor people abandoned out here with the shadow crawlies?"

They didn't grace him with an answer, just waited until those toothpaste-tube-sized fingers released Radio, then clicked the safety on.

They would find somewhere else to sleep tonight.

8
The Prize Bullet

Keep walking. The road snaked out into an abyssal horizon. Their ears held the ringing from the gunshot and the specks of the stars were all smeary. It got worse when they blinked. They blinked a lot.

Keep walking. The village had to be here somewhere. They wouldn't know until they were right on top of it. And what were the chances a shadow dweller would pick them off before they got to a house with a lock? Pretty high, they figured. They carried the gun out in the open to scare off the more fearful and the more intelligent ones, but eventually someone would take the risk.

Radio was certainly bolder now. It chose to walk next to True, just out of reach but unhidden.

"Are you really a shadow dweller?" they asked.

Radio walked a few paces without answering. It was too dark to make out the expression on its face, but eventually it lifted its hand, bobbed both its pointer finger and its head.

"Huh."

Well, that was... something.

"You've eaten people?"

Because that was what it meant to be a shadow dweller. That was what they chose over starvation. An even longer pause, then, nod the finger, nod the head.

"Huh." Too tired to do or say or think anything else.

They crested a hill. No sign of the village anywhere ahead. They clomped into a patch of woods. How much damn farther was this place? It felt like they had been on this road for six thousand years. They tripped over their own toes at the bottom of the hill. Good thing Radio was the only one there, technically. It couldn't tattle on them. It did tap their elbow and point to a car wrapped around a tree in the ditch, overgrown with weeds.

There was an idea. Out of sight, out of mind, right? It was better than nothing and more appealing than one single farther step on that cursed serpentine road.

A corpse had oozed corpse sludge all over h drivers' side and the stench of human broiled by the sun hung in the air so strong that even True could taste a hint of it. But the windows were all intact and the locks worked.

They crawled into the trunk and made themself comfortable. Glowing ribbons of soft green light flowed across the midnight sky. The northern lights dipped toward the dirty car and rilled back up. Wearily, True took everything out of their pack, checked it all, put it all back neatly. When their fingers brushed a crinkly chip bag, they hesitated. Trading those dentures for one boot and some licorice had seemed like a rookie mistake. But this was probably the last licorice they'd ever see. Better save it.

"Hey," they whistled to get Radio's attention. "No snacking on me while I sleep."

Radio held up its pinky finger, a promise. It switched. Middle finger. Jackass. Maybe they should kill it now, before it killed them. The idea flickered brief and bright. They couldn't trust a shadow dweller, they shouldn't let their guard down with one lingering below.

Then again, Radio'd had plenty of other opportunities to eat them.

A pack of coyotes started up their screechy howl somewhere west of the treeline. Comforting. True lay curled around their pack, their ear pressed to the thin floor of the trunk. They listened to the grass rustle as Radio nestled under the vehicle until they dropped suddenly, steeply, into sleep.

♪

Night shone through the windows when they startled awake. Very abruptly. Their hand flew o the gun before their brain finished powering on. Empty air. Rocket fuel shot into their sense. They jolted up. The thief pressed them down again, hand over their mouth, straddling them.

"You hush." Eliza's thin, scratchy voice accompanied her narrow face above them, framed by the open, broken moon roof. She held the gun in front of their face. "Move, and three of these bullet are going in your friend."

True bit their tongue until the sting and taste of iron kicked across their mouth. Eliza stared at them for several more seconds. At last, she lifted her hand. She made quick work of click-clacking all the parts of the gun that clicked and clacked. The magazine popped out. She wedged her pinky nail under a single bullet and slide it free. Left three behind. It glinted in the moonlight when she held it up. A brief, satisfied smile flitted across her chapped lips. She tucked the bullet into her pocket and slid the magazine home.

"Good listening," she said to True's glowering form. Stretching up, she shoved the gun in a crevice, out of reach. And, wordlessly, slid out the trunk and vanished into the night.

True stared after her long after the faint rustling of her retreat faded. Heart in their throat. Slowly, the sounds of the night returned. Crickets chirping, frogs croaking, the faint swish of nocturnal beasts creeping through the underbrush. Muted snoring. They peered down at the empty place where they'd last seen Radio. The grass cloaked it, but its snoring carried on. Exhaling long and slow out their nose, they leaned back on the wheel hub,

Get the gun.

Don't get the gun.

They flip-flopped the decision. Not that it should have been a decision. They needed to grab the gun before someone else snatched it, or it rained, or some other bullshit

In five seconds they would get it.

Five seconds.

Four.
Three.

9

The Season of the Witch

Finally, the damn village. It had been pathetically close to the car they'd made their bed. It was useless to spend energy grouching about it now, but they grouched anyway. On principal.

They passed a front lawn dotted with old graves. A season's worth of soft new wildflowers thrived over the mounds, soon they would overgrow the rocks True had placed as headstones. The village stood empty, a shell of a ghost town overrun with poplar saplings and a rampant raspberry bush. Its residents dead or gone and its remnants all looted in the earlier days. It didn't even have a name anymore. Some dumbass had robbed the town sign long before True had come along, and the place was too tiny to have a pinpoint on any map True had scoured. Although they knew generally where it would be based on bigger towns to the north and the east, so this place worked as a half decent map marker.

Not that they would admit it out loud, but they liked the place. They liked the quiet, the isolation. Nobody bothered to stop for long because everybody knew the village, like every other small town, village, hamlet, et cetera, had been cleaned out. Nobody bothered, except True, who stopped to bury a few more ex-residents whenever they passed through.

Not this time.

There, something to grouch about. They didn't have time to stop and dig muddy holes for a couple rotting corpses because the infernal Red Faction was trying to end the world. They hoofed a chunk of broken curb. Radio skittered out of the way of the formidable concrete missile.

"Don't get in the way," they grumbled, marching past it down the center road that had one been the village's main access, shopping district, and town square all in one. Tall elms spread wide branches over the roads, saplings filled the spaces between the older trees. The pollen irritated True's allergies, but on the east end of the village a house sat back from the road, with a yard dominated by a pine tree that suffocated the encroaching wildflowers under a thick blanket of pine needles, and when it rained the air felt fresher under its branches. True couldn't really smell the pine, but they pretended the could in those rare moments.

Like the graves, the pine house would have to wait for another day. They could only afford one stop in the village.

A gas station full of rust and broken window glass was losing the battle against local flora. Grass pushed cracks through the tile floor and a chokecherry tree swarmed the west wall of the squat, square building. True argued with a tangle of determined grass for access through the front door.

"I'll light you on fire," they threatened between sneezes. Out of the corner of their eye, Radio twitched and slinked off to do whatever it did when it wasn't hovering. They should have called it Whiitigo for all the skulking it did. Wiping their nose and accompanying hole, they wedged their way into the gas station and trampled a path all around the empty shelves.

The contents of erupted milk cartons coated the insides of the glass door refrigerators. Someone had been very careful to shut each door, trapping the colony of rot inside. Turning from that disaster, they kicked around under the front counter until they scrounged up a map. The paper was soft with age, grime yellowed the edges and faded the ink. But it was legible. Swiping off the counter with a crash, they flattened the map over it. Now, how were they getting to Vancouver.

That far west was out of their usual territory. They needed a way through the mountains, preferably a straight shot but they would settle for a winding highway if they had to. Their sense of direction was decent, but they weren't keen on getting lost in the great Canadian Rockies, what with all the great Canadian angry bears and the great Canadian miserable weather.

A swish and scrunch pulled their attention to the door. They reached for their shovel. If Linc or his goonies showed face in this village, True swore they would mash their noses in. Was it too much to ask for one put stop where something didn't go catastrophically wrong?

A kid popped into the station, shaking a tangle of grass from her ankle. It took her a beat to get free and look up, hair beads swishing around her chin. One of her eyes turned in, and the vision in her other eye must not have been great because it took her another beat to make out True. Then, of course, she screamed.

"Mom!" She fumbled a switchblade from her belt. "Shadow dweller!"

True groaned, eyes rolling. Children. The last thing they needed was an overprotective mom taking their head off over a case of mistaken identity.

A metal staff preceded the mother into the gas station. True levelled their shovel right back at her close-cropped curls.

The woman scanned them up and down, finally settling her gaze on the scar. Neither revulsion nor fear warped her expression, which was more than True expected.

"Friend or foe?" she asked, lingering on the scar.

"Neutral," True answered.

A second form materialized behind the woman, broader and roughly the same height. He nudged her.

"Look at the pack," he said into her ear.

The woman's gaze flicked over their pack, and, hesitantly, she drew back her staff to rest it on her muscled shoulder. A nice gesture, but it didn't do much to put True at ease. She was blocking the only exit.

"You must be brand new if you're looking through this place," she said.

True lifted a corner of the map for her to see. "Looking for a route."

"Where you headed?"

"Vancouver."

Recognition flickered over the woman's face. She bit her lip, and they could tell by the way her foot tapped on the buckled vinyl floor that she was weighing out a decision.

"We could get you out there," she offered, "depending on what's in that pack."

A trade. Now there was a language they could speak. Come to think of it, they hadn't traded their haul from the cul-de-sac. That left them decent stuff to negotiate with. And they could let themself by a little generous with it, the idea of hiking that extra weight across the mountains did not appeal to them.

"How fast can you get me there?"

"In a hurry?" the start of a laugh lightened the woman's question. It died under True's mirthless expression. "Fourteen days."

"Can you make it quicker?"

The levity returned, wry and teasing. "Twelve, if you can keep up."

"Twelve, then." True nodded, clipping their shovel to their pack. They motioned the strangers inside and took a moment to assess their clients. A woman, a man, and a beanpole of a half-grown child. Family unit, maybe? All with dark skin, bodies toughened by the elements, and hiking packs. All of their footwear was sturdy and well-worn. Traveller footwear. They noted the outline of a pendant under the man's grey shirt and pinholes in the woman's earlobes. That was as good a place as any.

"I've got earrings," they started, tapping the silver hoop in their own right ear. "Good quality."

"Clean?"

"Clean." If you counted 'plucked from a corpse and dumped straight into the bag' as clean. There was no visible gunk on them, anyways. Besides, they'd never known anyone to die from wearing corpse jewelry.

"What else?"

"What are you looking for?"

"Thread, sewing needles, bandages," the woman listed, "got any of those?"

"Dental thread," True offered.

"That'll do."

Negotiation continued for a few more minutes, the woman did most of the talking while the kid wobbled around the store plucking price tags off the shelves. She held the tags up to her good eye.

They settled on the dental floss, two pairs of good wool socks, a half skein of yellow yarn that had probably started to dry rot but at least wasn't infested, the matching knitting needles, three carabiners, and an empty metal bottle with a screw top.

"The west cost is a little far for a scavenger, eh?" the man spoke up. He had an accent they couldn't place. They leaned away as he bent his head over the old map. Crowds were one thing, they couldn't help getting bumped around once in a while. But they didn't have to like people in their space.

"You're going," True said.

"We are meeting with our caravan," the man replied.

"Know anything about the Faction over there?"

The man's head snapped up. At once, the civility the woman had been trying to hold up, dropped. Rocking back on her heels, she tapped her staff twice on the floor to catch the kid's attention.

"Kiari, outside."

In one fluid motion she had the end of the staff jammed under True's chin.

Shit, maybe they'd misjudged the group. A family, dressed for travel, on their way to a caravan. It screamed civilian. And True had never seen a factioneer as young as the kid, but maybe that was part of the disguise. The woman tipped her head, and the man broke from the counter, following the child out the door.

"Whatever your business with the Faction is, we don't want any part of it," the woman said. Not factioneers, then. True's fingers lifted slowly to the staff, curled around it. They kept their other hand out where she could see it, displaying their empty palm.

"They're killing people," they said when they were sure the staff wouldn't kick into their throat when they spoke.

"We know. We're staying out of it. Whatever new world order they're trying to pull, it's not our business."

"It will be when there's none of us left to feed you."

The woman shook her head, lowering her staff. "If we stick out necks out there won't be any of us left to feed, and I have a daughter to protect.

True bit their tongue, considering. "The Faction is going after civs now?"

That was new. Until two days ago, even the violence against scavengers had been limited. True was under the impression that the Red Faction needed civilians on their side. Everyone needed civs. Just like everyone needed scavengers to fuel the After Market, and everyone needed the After Market to bolster the market, and everyone needed, however reluctantly, the Faction to act as healers. They were all cogs in a closed system, one part couldn't mangle another part without collapsing the whole machine.

But maybe the Faction wanted that.

"Not exactly, but there have been an awful lot of suspicious disappearances lately." The woman flipped her staff onto her shoulder and moved to exit.

"Wait," True called. When the woman hesitated, they pulled a highlight from a dust-coated mug by the register. "I'll give you everything we agreed on if you show me the quickest way to Vancouver on the map."

The woman drummed her fingers on her staff.

"I have some chocolate, too," they added reluctantly. It was basically robbery, considering the woman had been ready to walk them there herself a minute ago.

"Fine," she said, plucking the highlighter from their hand. Bending over the map, she started tracing. "You're awfully determined to start shit with the Faction."

"Yeah, well, they killed a merchant I liked."

The woman gave them a look that felt like an x-ray peeling back all the layer of bloodshed that had soaked into their skin those past few days. She popped the highlighter cap. The path was traced, the goods handed over.

"Good luck," she said as parting words. She sounded like she meant it.

True was busy studying the highlighter path marked on the map when Radio drifted in. It dangled a length of springy black fabric in front of their nose.

"What's this?" They took the fabric. It was soft to the touch and formed a tube. Radio motioned to the lower half of its face. Oh, a mask.

The fabric rested gently on the line where their bandana had dug in.

"Thank you," they said. They passed it a pair of socks.

Radio drew a bumpy bubble in the dust on the dead computer monitor and pointed to the door, a questioning look on its face.

"Travellers, I traded for directions." True answered. They peered over the top of their new mask a Radio while it bent to examine the map. A question rolled on their tongue. They hadn't forgotten last night. Radio was a shadow dweller, a monster. The thing children hid under the covers from.

But they hadn't forgotten yesterday morning, either.

"Are you coming with me?" The enemy of their enemy was their friend, that was the saying, wasn't it?

It tilted its head a smidge. They mirrored it. Once, they would have mistaken its gaze as vacant. An easy mistake to make, with eyes that black and lonely, and a face that seemed to forget emotion. But they could see the sharpness there now. The way it studied, not stared.

"It'll be dangerous." They added, memories of Radio effortlessly dislocating Eliza's arm flashing through their head. "I know stalking me is your thing, but I'm sure you can find another ugly bastard to follow around. Maybe one who gets blown up less."

Radio shook its head, a wry smile fighting for a place on its lips. It held out a fist, waited for True to touch their knuckles to its.

Well, that was settled then.

"We're gonna die," True said, picking up the map. Radio lost its battle with the grin.

10
The Consequences of Punching a Bear

Seven days in, travel was simultaneously much faster than their usual pace, since they weren't stopping to harvest, and agonizingly slow. It got a little less mind-numbing when they made it out of the plains, but navigating the mountains slowed their progress. And it rained. A lot. A mist of grey rain stuck to their skin and turned the terrain slick, running in rivulets down their legs and filling up their heavy boots.

They were off the highways, on a stretch of the highlighter trail between the roads and a town that marked the halfway point. Kiari's mother had added a tiny note that read 'take the deer paths'. Of which there were about five thousand. Winding through the trees, breaking apart in clearings and re-forming as three new paths on the other side. But the trails were easier to traverse than the rest of the untamed landscape and they all ran the same general direction.

True craned their neck to squint at the clouded sky. Thin, sprinkly rain caught on their eyelashes, forcing them to blink. It was hard to tell what time it was with the sun behind a curtain of gauze, but their stomach said noon.

They tossed their pack under the tree with the widest dry circle around the trunk and scooted under to settle beside it. Relief cramped their sore feet, and they were too tired to mind how the back scratched their back. Pulling out their dried meat, they skimmed the surroundings for Radio.

In spite of their shaky agreement to travel together, it drifted in and out of perception in fields of tall grass and between the tall black trees. True was making a game out of how long they took to spot it. Zero points if it made it to the fireside first.

Scan left, nothing. Scan right, nothing. Not unusual. They tried again, slower, more attentively. Still nothing to the left, but there, downhill and to the right of a fat oak. Or maple, or whatever the hell. *Gotcha*. They flicked a pine needle at it.

The mass shifted. Huge, black... huger, way too huge. Damn, the bridge of their nose scrunched, not Radio after all.

They watched the bear's rump wobble over the bush, apprehension curdling in their stomach. Setting their lunch to the side, they leaned forward to get a better eye on the surroundings. That bear was a little too close for comfort, although it snuffled farther from them as the second passed. An image of Radio turning into a bear snack made an entrance stage right of their brain. How would they know. It didn't scream. Did it?

Plastic crinkled, sending a thrill of goosebumps up their arm.

Zero points, they thought, relaxing back into the shelter of the tree branches. They bopped Radio without looking. Without thinking. It knew better than to touch their stuff. Their fingers brushed fur. The plaintive yowl of a miffed bear cub right beside their ear shot ice through their veins.

It seemed almost impossible how fast mama bear wheeled around, a snarl curling her muzzle, fangs bared and dripping. True didn't stick around to contemplate the physics of it.

"Why couldn't you have been a bunny?" they hissed as they scrambled from under the tree. Foot slipping. Rain in their eyes. Adrenaline spiked every sense at the rumble of mama bear's bellow and the thunder of her galloping towards them.

Of all the stupid things. They cursed themself out, hurtling fallen trees and dodging upright ones at a dead sprint. Twigs gouged their clothes and bark scraped their skin. Never in a million years could they outrun a bear. They couldn't stop running either. Stop running, die. Keep running, die anyways. Why were those always the choices they got dealt?

Their heavy soles fought for traction on the wet forest floor until, abruptly, it wasn't there.

The forest hadn't thinned out or stopped a significant distance from the edge of the cliff. Instead, the stubborn fir trees had dug their roots down into rocky earth and left nothing but a sharp drop to certain death hidden beyond their branches. True plummeted.

Their ribs hit the ledge hard and scraped all the way up to their armpits. Fingernails split as they dug them into the dirt, desperately trying to keep from slipping off. They probably yelped but they couldn't hear it over the sound of imminent death and their heart thundering in their ears.

"Fuck," they gasped, "fuckfuck*fuck*." They slipped another inch. Above them, the bear snuffled and snorted.

Which was worse, getting mauled by a bear or falling of the ledge?

They didn't look down, they couldn't. They pressed every square inch of them as tight as physically possible to the face of the cliff. The fall was worse, definitely the fall.

Another slip, miniscule, so their fingers curled into claws, were their only anchor. Suddenly there was no air for their heaving lungs. They dared a peek down. Maybe there was an exposed root, or another ledge, or anything. Anything. Dizzying vertigo slammed into them. Squeezing their eyes shut, they will themself to mould to the cliff face. Fuck, they were *really high up*.

They braced themself on razor thin footholds and convinced the fingers of their left hand to uproot, one by one. Bear or no bear, they had to get back on the ledge. They got down to the last finger, stretching the other in anticipation of the next step, when the chunk of rock holding their weight from below gave out.

If they'd had any air left they would have screamed. Their right hand—their last anchor—ripped from the ledge and they plunged.

An eternity and less than a second later they jolted to a halt. Two black-clad hands gripped their arm.

Through much heaving and hauling on limbs that felt like rubber, they ended up back on top of the ledge. Hands, knees, solid ground. A scream bubbled to their tongue, and the urge to laugh, and the urge to scream more swelling with it. But they settled for digging their fingers into the dirt until the hysteria passed.

When the need to scream eased off, they stood. Wobbled, sank back to their knees. That was a negative for walking, then. They glanced over at Radio, seated well within arms-reach and flushed from the effort of pulling them off the cliff. It watched them closely, as always.

"I'm not a fan of heights," they said.

Clearing their sore throat, they scraped together the remnants of their wits and forced themself to their feet. It was time to get back to their pack, before another bear cub decided to munch on it.

"What did you do with the bear?" True asked, glimpsing the forest ahead. At least they wouldn't have to worry about getting lost. A path of broken twigs and crushed foliage marked their flight from the bear.

Radio wiggled its fingers.

"That's not really an answer."

That earned them a heavy sigh and a heavier tap on the elbow. Radio held Galya's gun by the barrel, offering it back to them. Oh, good, they were down a bullet. Or several. They decided to leave the matter. Whatever it had done, had worked, they were happy to leave it at that.

It took a while, but eventually the pack came into view. And so did its contents, strewn from the epicenter under the tree and halfway to Timbuktu. So much for a quick lunch. They stalled, surveying the damage. Bit down on a gnarled, hideous feeling that burrowed into their marrow. That was their home. That was all they had in the world.

A feather-light touch pulled them out of the spiral. Radio brushing the back of its hand against the back of theirs as it walked deeper into the wreckage, skimming all the bits of their very private life that had been thrown out in the daylight for anyone to see. It came to a stop, crouched, and resurfaced holding something up. Light glinted off the sewing needle. Good, they were going to need it, judging by the look of everything else. They pinched a dark blue thread from the fringe of their sash and worked it loose.

It took precious time to gather all the scraps and pieces, following scattered trails and scrounging up on branches and under bushes. More time yet to stitch shut the gashes in their bag with sore fingers and a rain slick needle.

"Anything you need..." they hesitated with the word on the tip of their tongue and their tongue poking at the hole where their missing tooth lined up with the cleft in their lip. There were some difficult words in the English language, and they couldn't think of an easier way to say this one.

"Stitched." It came out mangled, and they held up the threaded needle in case Radio had a hard time understanding them. It shook its moppy head and made a motion like it was pushing them away with the back of its hand.

"What is that?" True mimicked the motion. Radio tipped its head in consideration, its fingers hover in the air, playing an imaginary piano. Finally, it reached down and traced a word in the dirt.

Sign.

It waited for True to skim the word, then wiped it away and traced a new one.

No.

It repeated the pushing motion. It added another word below the first.

Yes.

It pointed to the sky, then traced a line down. Yes and no. True copied the motions.

"Is there one for this?" They held up the needle and thread. After some consideration, Radio held its left hand out flat and made as if running the needle of its right hand through its skin.

Yes, no, stitching. True made the motion. An easier word. They tried all the signs again.

"Got any more?"

It shrugged.

"Teach me?" they asked. "I'll trade...earrings?" It was a weak trade, and they knew it, but admittedly they didn't have much to trade. They'd handed over a lot for the map, and lost some to the wildlife. And they didn't know the kind of thing Radio would want. They'd never paid attention to the things it foraged, never seen it inside the Market.

In answer to their offer, it pulled back its hair to show off its unpierced ear. The high collar of its poncho shifted, revealing a glimpse of pink scar. There and gone, Radio smoothing its hair and shirt back in place.

"Teeth?" True tried. Teeth didn't sell great, but Radio seemed strange enough to want them. Cannibalism and all that. Maybe teeth made good snacks. Like extra crunchy popcorn.

No. Hand pushed. It smeared the words on the dirt patch and traced a new one.

Free. The motion it made was a little more complex than the others.

The gnarled feeling crawled back over True's skin, trailing with it the same dull pain under their solar plexus that they had been ignoring since the firs blown-up After Market. Biting their tongue, they stuck the needle in their bag. Shut it. Stood.

"Come on, I don't want to lose any more daylight." They stamped out the word written in the dirt.

That wasn't the way things worked, there was no such thing as getting something for free. Not between strangers. Not even between friends, and True certainly didn't have any of those left. There were only people who wanted to kill them, and people who mostly didn't.

They pulled up their mask. Glancing back at the pine, they saw only forest. The place where Radio had been, now empty.

11
The Healing Properties of Spring Water

From miserable drooling rain to killer sweltering heat in one day. Their body made it own rain as they trudged. Sweat, sweat, and more sweat. At this point they had given up on ever being dry again, and their side hadn't quit burning since their slide down the cliff face.

They lifted their water bottle to their chapped lips. The last warm dregs sloshed at the sides of the canteen. They slowed, ears and eyes piqued. They were in the mountains. Well, big foothills. There had to be running water somewhere. Wasn't that what mountains were? Big rocks, always have water running down them? They kept walking, searching for a source of water.

At least they didn't have to keep an eye out for the bear. They'd passed a suspicious brown lump flopped on the forest floor, a swarm of flies forming at the root of a dried river of blood caking the fur around its hindquarters. Of course, they hadn't gone near the thing. They weren't about to lose a limb poking a bear twice. But the had held their breath for the world's longest minute while the bear-lump gave not the faintest hint of motion or noise.

Delicate burbling caught their attention. They split from the deer path and marched towards the sound, snapping twigs to mark their trail as they went. It wasn't far before they came to a stream of shallow, crystal water rushing over a bed of time-smoothed stones. They couldn't have asked for a better source. Mother nature was smiling on them today. They scrubbed a trickle of sweat from their brow before it dripped in their eye. Okay, maybe Mother Nature was close-lipped grimacing at them, but they would take it.

The source of the burbling was a little ways upstream, where a rise in the land had created a miniature waterfall. A basin fed the stream. Crouching, True dipped their bottle in. Cool water rushed over their sore fingers, soothing, whisking away old blood and sweat and the heat of the day. A sigh escaped them before they caught it. Their bottle filled, but they lingered, indulging the feeling.

Biting the tip of their tongue, they clocked the water beyond the tiny waterfall. Ages worth of dirt and sweat, merchant's blood, stranger's blood, their blood, caked on their skin. In every crevice and pore. Would it kill anyone if they stopped here for an hour or two?

Knowing the Faction, probably. But the Faction was also probably going to kill them when they got to Vancouver, so they climbed the rise in the land and shrugged off their pack.

First things first, they put their shoes and socks up high. They had all the blisters they could manage. With their bag also out of the immediate splash zone, they plunged into the frigid water.

Two steps in and the bottom dropped from mid-shin to elbow-deep. Icy water seared the open scrapes on what had to be more than half their skin at this point. They sank and dipped their head back to drench their hair. Ugh, that felt better than anything had any right to feel.

Retreating back to the bank, they dug a lump of tallow soap from their pack, making a note to re-sort it. They'd stuffed everything in haphazardly earlier and nothing was where it was supposed to be. Stripping, they scrubbed as much of the grit and the grime for their ragged clothes as possible. Sullied water flushed from them like toxic run-off from the factories of old. Relieved of a thick layer of dirt, the ragged clothes looked even more threadbare.

"Even feels lighter," they joked to themself as they hung the clothes over some branches. A breeze raised goosebumps across their brown skin as they returned to the basin to scrub the layers of dirt from themself. Clear water, cool and tranquilizing wrapped around them like silk. Inviting them deeper. They obliged, sinking to their chin and letting their eyes slide closed. Everything was calm. Quiet. Nothing but the slow rush of water on their skin. Nothing but the silver burble of the waterfall and the hush of the breeze through the leaves. And a twig snapping on the shore.

Their eyes flew open and they whirled, half-rising from the water. Stones grinding underfoot and threatening to give way to a twisted ankle if they weren't treated with more respect.

Radio's moppy head and raggedy clothes loomed on the bank. If ever there was a perfect time to strike, this was it. True, naked and freezing, out of reach of any of their stuff. An instant of vulnerability from which they could not recover.

Radio waved, they waved back.

Okay, maybe not. Maybe it was judging them for their break. Silent judgement. The best kind because they didn't have to listen to any whining. True sank back into the basin, wondered how it handled the heat in what looked like seventy layers of black clothes.

Closing their eyes, they resumed their moment of relaxation in the midst of the second end of the world. Except now they were hyperaware of the person on the bank. They rubbed their breastbone, passing off the ache there as a consequence of falling off a cliff and pressed all the air from their lungs to sink lower. The water lapped treacherously close to their cleft. They tilted their head back, knew from experience that water up the nose burned like an acid shot to the brain.

A plip of water struck their ear, breaking them out of the spiral. They turned to scowl at Radio only to be met with a squirt of water in the face. A sharp gasp escaped them. They smacked water at it, drenching it. Instead of backing off, it gave them a sly grin and launched a wave at them. Ice cold, acid burning, straight to the face.

They jerked away, the stones shifted and betrayed their foot, and suddenly they were plunging underwater.

Son of a bitch!

Fire scorched the inside of their face.

"You—you—!" their own coughing kept interrupting them. They settled for shooting it the dirtiest glare they could muster, only for the glare to fade at the sight of Radio mid-silent-cackle. Head thrown back, eyes scrunched shut.

"You're evil," they sputtered out finally, and stalked back to the shallow ledge. Radio slinked through the basin like a crocodile, just eyes and a nose gliding around in circles, at first, then towards True. They prodded it away with their toe. It poked a finger out of the water and traced a tear down its face. True rolled their eyes and went back to getting lost in the web of branches that swayed overhead.

Once-smothering heat now warmed the chill out of their sore muscles. They almost didn't notice when Radio sloshed out of the water and wandered off. Definitely didn't notice it had come back until it beaned them in the back of the head with a pinecone.

"I'm beginning to think you pulled me off that cliff just to—" they lurched out of the way of a pink and brown streak in the nick of time. Water exploded from the basin, dousing them. Radio stayed under. Stayed so long that True leaned over to get a better look at its dark shape in the water in case it had done something incredibly stupid like crack its skull on the rocks.

Radio sprang from the bottom of the basin and soaked them all over again.

And laughed.

Caught off-guard, True slipped and went crashing face-first into the ice acid water. Radio caught them. Well, it caught their forehead and half gave them whiplash. But it was better than drowning, and Radio laughed more. Scratchy from unuse and bubbling like the waterfall over the stub of its tongue.

"I didn't know you could do that," they said.

Radio shrugged.

It made sense though, its tongue was gone, not its vocal cords. They'd just never heard it before. Not much laughing to be done these days. Not much laughing to be done around True in general. Maybe that was something they should change. Then again, what would be the point if they were marching to their death in a few days anyways.

But it was nice to hear now, from the stalker. A small, private smile spread on their broken lips. Sloshing out of the water, they trudged to their pack and set about re-packing it.

Radio climbed out of the basin. Late afternoon sun glittered off the droplets clinging to its hair and ropes of thick pink burn scars binding its skin. Chest, back, arms, some spread down its buttocks to the backs of its knees. All bulging and puckered. It looked like it hurt. True turned away.

Their fingers brushed a rumpled old chip bag and they drew it out, debating.

Ah, what the hell. They had a bad feeling about what was waiting for them in Vancouver, and they'd be pissed if they died without getting to eat their candy.

"Licorice?" they offered, plunking down at the water's edge. Radio gave them a questioning look. "Trade it for a question," they clarified, holding out the open end of the bag.

Radio fished a length of sticky soft candy out.

"Cheers." They clinked each other's licorice, though it wasn't a clink so much as a squelch. Mouth-watering sugar dissolved on their tongue with a burst of cherry flavour. They held the licorice in their mouth, letting it melt slowly. Giving their mouth time to adjust to the shock.

Out of all the things they missed from before the end of the world, sugar topped the list.

"What happened?" they asked, motioning to a patch of scar.

All the calm leeched out of Radio, it drew its knees up to its chest as if it could hide the marks. True bit the inside of their cheek. Way to kill the mood.

"You don't have to answer." They'd traded a question, not an answer, technically.

It got to its feet and abandoned the water's edge. There went that conversation. They were good at making conversations dead. Usually a lot quicker than this. Faintly they registered the soft thump of its footsteps approaching. A poke to their shoulder as Radio sat next to them and held out a scrap of fabric. A patch, the edges frayed and the silver embroidery faded. They didn't recognize the design, but the text read Canada, National Defence, Fire Services, in English and French.

"That yours?" True asked.

Radio nodded. Setting the little piece of its past on its lap, it reached down to the sand.

Couldn't shout. It wrote. Left behind.

True bit back a wince, their brain seizing the opportunity to remind them of Galya's final moments.

"That's fucked," they said.

Radio blew out a long exhale and shrugged, which could have meant anything. It picked at a loose thread on the patch, tension bundled up in its shoulders. Its black eyes held a distant glaze.

"Did you talk when you were a firefighter or just grunt?"

Radio punched them.

"Ow! Yeah, keep rolling your eyes." They flicked water at it. "You just told me your whole tragic backstory and I don't even know your name. I bet you never zipped your lip before."

The calm seeped back into it as it wrote the next word in the sand.

Name.

True watched it move its hands, fingers curled into a new shape. They motioned for it to repeat the sign, tilting their head to get a better look.

"That's gonna take me a minute to learn." They offered another licorice stick as an apology. Radio didn't seem to mind.

Later, clothes clean, pack re-ordered, and salve applied to the tract of torn-up skin that stretched from armpit to hip, they were on their way. Radio had spent the rest of its time gathering fistfuls of tiny purple flowers on long stalks and fastening them upside down to the back of its poncho with grass blades. True chose not to question it. Though they couldn't tell if the flowers were useful or decorative. They suspected it was useful.

By the time the sun had set, the tiny purple flowers were wilted, and the forest gave way to ancient asphalt. On the horizon, lit by the half moon and the dying flow of an expired sunset, were the frames of buildings. A village, the last stop between where'd they'd come from and where they were going. It looked like they were closer to Vancouver than they thought.

12
The Body in the Ditch

A chill had settled into the air and a blanket of stars lit the sky and the thin spiral of smoke rising from a single house on the tiny block. True eyed it as they got closer, weighing the possibilities. Sleeping inside was safest, but that village was toy-sized and if they had to break in the noise would echo. They didn't want to attract attention from whoever was making camp.

The shadows welcomed them into the forest. Leaf-heavy branches blotting out the stars and the sliver of smoke. Twigs crunched underfoot, for once they cursed their steel toes. There really was no sneaking in these things.

Radio crept along to their right, a thing of shadows itself.

"What do you think?" They turned to Radio, who squinted at the coils of smoke. A shrug. "Helpful."

A light kick in the ankle.

"If you break my leg, I'll die in these mountains, and you'll have no one to hound."

An evil grin creeped over Radio's face, and it mimed eating a corncob. True's eyes widened a fraction.

"You wouldn't." But the look Radio gave them didn't fill them with confidence. Neither did the fact they hadn't seen it eat anything except licorice the entire hike. It caught them staring and licked its lips theatrically. Spooky little shit. They shot it a scowl and pulled ahead.

A wet squelch interrupted their less-than-silent sneaking. Gore splattered the underbrush, red dumped out on the earth from a cavernous open abdomen. Dark skin. A small pendant. True recognized the man from the gas station.

Damn, they wondered if the other two were nearby, too. Faint wisps of steam rose from the eviscerated man. He hadn't been dead long. True frowned at him, something wasn't right about that picture. They crouched to get a better look, running a finger over the slippery flayed abdominal skin. The cut was too smooth to be animal.

What the hell.

His guts had been turned into a soup bowl. All the thick tubes branching from purpled organs had been sliced open and sluiced the last remnants of his blood into a pool cupped between his hips and ribs. They were no doctor, but they were pretty sure organs weren't supposed to free float.

Radio tapped their shoulder. Brow furrowed, it waved its hand over its temple, then point to the dead man.

A fresh welt puffed up his face from the ridge of his brow to the corner of his eye. True squinted at it, tilting the man's chin to catch the gauzy moonlight better.

"Does that look like a lion to you?" Apprehension thrummed in their veins as they unclipped their shovel. Habitually, they jammed the tip into the soft red earth. The first scoop of dirt out of the thousands it took to dig a grave.

A piercing wail split the night air. True stopped dead. The scream could have belonged to a fox, or a coyote, except they knew the dead man had been travelling with a kid. They threw eyes first to the village where the scream had risen from, then to Radio.

The wailing had cut off by the time they reached the village. The crunch of metal striking wood led them to the one house in the entire village with smoke curling out of its chimney. The front door's lock had been mangled, someone banged around inside. True skirted the house, clomping into the backyard and straight into the path of a short woman with a heavy bat.

She cracked them between the eyes, knocking them back with a shower expletives. They had the good sense to keep peddling backwards in spite of the instant, blinding migraine. Got the shovel up, barricade. Blinked away the fireworks in the nick of time to see the bat careening down on them, Otsana's white streak glowing in the moonlight at the other end of it. Her bat struck their shovel but the blow glanced, ripped off its trajectory.

Radio slammed Otsana into the side of the house with an audible whud. With a quick twist she'd cracked the butt of her bat into its jaw. She was fast, they'd give her that. They flipped their shovel to fill the gap. For once the odds were in their favour despite the blood trickling down that face. Two against one, and Radio knew how to fight.

That thought came a second too soon. Cold hands shoved them from behind. Their forehead scraped off rough splintered fencing. They whirled, shovel whipping. The blade winged the shover, a narrow miss. And who stood before them but a greasy, quivering cook.

"Jonesy.'" The snarl dropped out of them, blood running into their scar, over their teeth. They could practically see the chill run the course of Jonesy's spine. He hadn't expected to see them any more than they'd expect to see him. Blanching, he crammed his fingers into his pits, turned, bolted.

A crunch and the clink of glass shattering dragged True back to the original fight. They spit blood and returned to the backyard to see Otsana smashing her heel on a black lump and launching it through a basement window.

The clatter of Radio landing smothered their approach. They cracked her clean on the back of the head, returning that static she'd gifted them earlier. She crumpled, and they wasted no time whacking her again. Stripping the hem off her shirt, they looped it about her wrists and ankles. Shoddy workmanship, at best. They just needed it to stall her until they came back.

They ducked to peer into the basement. The narrow window sat too high on the basement wall, and the moonlight shone too soft to break the darkness inside.

"Are you dead?" True whispered.

The tips of Radio's fingers poked over the ledge.

"Meet me upstairs."

The back door was locked. No key under the doormat, but a rock solved that issue. A quick jiggle and slap in the dark and they were in.

It was as cool in the house as it was outdoors. A hum filled the air, but not the acrid sting of smoke. The ghostly spiral above the house wasn't from a fire, then. Mud marked a path on the kitchen tile from whoever had been stomping around earlier. The counters were clear, and the glass-faced cabinets had been stuffed full of red and white packets. True skimmed the labels.

Who the hell needed four thousand blood testing kits? The sink was spotless, suspiciously so.

The humming seemed louder on one side of the kitchen, and True crept toward it, hoping to find what, exactly, they weren't sure. A basement door would be nice. They clipped the edge od a dingy yellow fridge and stopped to shine their lighter over it. No graffiti, no paper, but smears of crusted brown decorated the handle.

What were the chances?

Squoosh.

Light. Now *that* was terrifying.

A single, bare bulb cast yellow light on the kitchen from the depths of a cold fridge. Unnatural and sickly, cold like the air all around it. Nothing like the oily light from the kerosene lamps or the warm flicker of firelight that True had grown accustomed to. It burned afterimages on their retinas. Talk about spooky. Nobody used electricity anymore, half the grids in the country had been shut down when the power companies ran out of employees, the other half were lost to damage and disuse.

"What the hell,'" they whispered.

Small coolers filled the bottom two shelves. All red and white. All marked with a letter and a plus or minus symbol. A tray sat on the top shelf, filled with tiny hollow plastic straws like the one Otsana had held their stolen blood in. Seized by a horrible curiosity, they popped one of the coolers and stared, lips pressed together, at the contents. Blood bags. They poked one, felt their stomach flop in time with the sloshing of the blood against the plastic.

Really? That's what got them? They pressed an annoyed arm to their belly.

Something hefty hit the floor down the hall, rocking their brain back into motion. Right, screaming kid, creepy factioneers, somebody in the house with them.

The hum of the fridge set their hackles on end as they crept down the hall, wiggling the handles of the doors. All locked. Except, as if they needed any more warning that they were not alone, the door at the end. That one hung half-open, a squat bulbous silhouette lay in wait beyond it.

Nerves drove them forward. They struck the door fast, shovel arcing.

Dark skin, cropped hair, glittering earrings. They recognized the lump an instant before their shovel connected. Luckily, she was fast. The collision of metal shovel with metal staff sent vibrations up their arm with a resounding clang.

Shovel dropped, both hands up. The civilian woman jabbed her staff across the cramped space and knocked True square in the chin. They staggered back.

"Wait, wait!" What the hell had the woman's name been? "Kiari's mom."

She gave them time to yank down their mask and spit out the blood pooling in their mouth.

"Scavenger." Sweat flecked her hard face, her breath came in shallow bursts. She didn't sound happy to see them. Given the staff in their face, the feeling was mutual. "Where the hell is my daughter?"

"I don't have her."

"Why should I believe you?"

"Do your eyes work?" Oh, real bright idea, smart mouth. The bathroom tile bounced back the echo of their teeth clacking shut. Silence followed, briefly. Skimming the empty hall behind True, the woman dropped her staff from their jaw. Her eyes did work after all. The empty hall must have dislodged all her panic from wherever she'd been stuffing it because her breath spasmed in in in but never out.

"Hey." They kicked her shin in hopes it would flip her exhale switch. It did. She snapped into motion, stalking past them.

"Check the basement, I'm checking upstairs. If you find her shout for me, for Suni. Suni Valdivia—Valdivia?" It all came out at once on the tail of her exhale. For approximately half a second her gaze skirted over True to make sure they were keeping up.

"Valdivia," they repeated, poking their head in to make sure everything was straight. "True Gallows."

"Gallows," she said, then vanished around the corner.

They rocked back on their heels, their skin prickling. The bathroom was spotless. An uneasy sensation settled in the pit of their stomach. No curtain on the tub, no flecks of dried water on the mirror, not a speck of dust. They got the idea that if they had a sense of smell this place would reek of old bleach. The only hint of dirt in the entire, white-tiled room was a thin brown line wedged into the cracked caulk at the lip of the tub and a splatter of searingly bright red blood on one of the tiles. Eye level. Like someone had been thrown against the wall.

They hoped that kid was in the basement. Radio probably wouldn't eat a child. Probably. It would definitely eat a kidnapper first.

A quick check under the sink revealed roughly eight thousand half-empty bottles of every cleaner imaginable jammed tight, stacked on top of each other. They glimpsed a candy blue slime trail leading from the cap of one bottle and warded off the sudden, strange urge to lick it.

A ghost tapped their elbow, ducking just in time to avoid a shovel to the head. The edge embedded in the wall, sending a reverberant clunk through the bones of the house.

"You'll never learn," True grumbled, prying the shovel free. Radio retreated, wraithlike, behind a newly open hall door.

A rusted butter knife lay discarded on the hardwood where Radio had jimmied the basement door. The hum of electricity rose from beyond shadowed stairs, warning them off.

The meager moonlight only braved the first couple steps before abandoning the rest to pitch dark. Too dark for their eyes to adjust, though they blinked a couple times before pulling out their lighter. The ring of light hit Radio and a scrawny pile of limbs armed with a knife that it was failing to coax from the bottom step. Every move it made resulted in a swipe from a pathetically small blade clutched in pathetically small hands. A long red tube snaked from one skinny arm and into the dark.

Okay, kid found. Rescue side quest over. Except nothing could ever be that simple. Radio's head ratcheted toward the basement depths, the rest of its body followed. Tense, it stood between the kid and whatever it had heard, and motioned True further down the steps.

The gun sat heavy in their waistband. For emergencies, they told themself. No need to go around wasting bullets. Valdivia's name was on their tongue. Let her come pry her spawn off the creepy basement steps of the creepy too-clean house. The minute she got down here they were getting the hell out of dodge.

Pale arms rose out of the cavernous black of the basement and plucked Radio from the steps.

13
The Dark Basement

True thundered down the stairs, missing half the steps. Their trusty lighter wavered but held and cast thin light on the basemen. Stained floor, rust or blood leading to a drain under the bulb. Narrow drag marks cut through the stains.

And bodies.

Row after row of naked, sallow bodies swayed upside down from rusted chains. The back of the basement was lit, a second fridge hanging wide open to spotlight an IV, a blood bag, and two thrashing shapes.

Hrōkr towered over Radio, pinning it to a freezer. A hand wrapping a rusted chain tight around its neck, the other pressing a sleek black gun to its head. Wide, mirthless grin stretch over their bone-coloured maw. Horrendous wet sandpaper choking rang off the concrete wall.

"Hrōkr!" True hooked the gun from their waistband. The scarecrow of a medic swivelled to shine their grin and gun on True. Fire spit through the basement. True lurched out of the bullet's path, skipping the last stair. They pitched to miss stomping on the screaming kid, a wrenched muscle raking them from shoulder to hip. Hrōkr cocked their head. Ran their tongue over their teeth. Got halfway through the motion when a bullet took care of the rest of the teeth. True's finger shivered on the triggered.

Red misted the air, and the kickback burned all the way across their chest. Hrōkr was nothing but red. True saw nothing but red. They tossed the gun, without a break in their stride kicked the collapsing body down and for good measure stomped on the remnants of Hrōkr's skull. Wet squelches filled the basement.

They were about *sick* of these entitled jackasses eviscerating their life.

A final squelch and they stumbled back, bumping into one of the many cold bodies. They needed to catch their breath. The air tasted of rust.

"Radio?" They wheezed. Their side screamed where they'd pulled that muscle. Not surprising, not important. Pushing themself upright deleted their vision.

They blinked away stars to see red-stained hands reached for them. Radio, unharmed. Good, a ball of nerves unravelled from their stomach.

It pitched forward to—catch True? When had they started falling? It pressed their pulled side muscle.

Fuck that hurt. Shoved its hand away with gritted teeth. Fridge light glinted off shiny fresh blood on its palm. Glancing down.

"Shit," breathless, "oops."

The hand returned, pressing hard on the epicenter of the spreading lake of blood that stained their shirt.

Not a pulled muscle.

Hrōkr's gun drooled a lazy curl of smoke. The light flickered out.

14
The Doctor and Eliza

...

...

...

There was mold on the popcorn ceiling. True stared at it a while before it occurred to them that they were alive and in horrific pain. The next step on the agenda was a groan, which did not make the pain any better but did give them an ounce of satisfaction for acknowledging the pain.

Next order of business was to move. They appeared to be in a bathtub with one leg slung over the side, the other halfway up the wall, and their head on the tub floor. They tried to sit up. Emphasis on tried. Two things happened at once then. One, a fountain of molten agony jetted from their gut into every crevice of their body. Two, burn-scarred hands pushed them down.

They found their tongue too dry and heavy to speak, but managed to curl their fingers into a weak approximation of Radio's name. They were weak. Worse, they were vulnerable. The scarred hands found theirs, squeezed.

Okay, okay. They let their eyes slip closed while they processed. Things were starting to seep back into the fat cotton ball that had replaced their brain. Ugh, it even hurt to think. Screeching from a metal hellbeast bent on their destruction—creaky hinges—wreaked havoc on their pounding head.

"I heard noise and I know you didn't make it. Is Sleeping Beauty awake or just gassy?"

True mustered the strength to unfurl their middle finger and aim it at the voice. Probably not the brightest idea, pissing of the person whose bathtub they were recovering in.

They pressed the sorest spot on their aching body. A rough line split their flesh below their ribs and above the wool of their sash. Stitches. Their cotton ball brain began to spit out some more information. A thump rattled the out-facing side of the tub.

"Calm your tits, sis," the unfamiliar voice muttered. True pried their crusty eyes open, hand closing around an imaginary shovel handle. "That woke you up. Come on, sunshine, struggle a little more. There you go."

The voice belonged to a pointy, shadowed face, attached to a spindly body that half draped over Radio.

"Eliza," True said, thin and slow. They'd worked up just enough saliva for it. Eliza flashed a mouthful of yellowed teeth that had been filed into points. The smile, if it could be called a smile, dropped when Radio shoved her off.

"Rude." She flicked a long dark tangle of her shoulder. "Anyway, I was only waiting to make sure Allsaint did what he said he'd do, and he did. He's a real doctor, you know, used to be one of the best. You're welcome. See ya."

"Wait." That was too many words to process at once.

Eliza swung out the open door. "You'll figure it out on your own."

"You... Linc..."

Eliza flopped back into frame. A wide, wide smile stretched her cracked lips apart until they split. Blood trickled over her pointed teeth as she mimed a gun to her head. A roach scurried up the doorframe beside her.

"Linc's dead." She slapped the bug flat under her fist and tossed it into her mouth. Pale yellow slime jetted from behind her teeth with a crunch. "You're not, I don't like owing people. Go away."

She vanished then, hopefully to never be seen again. True shifted their focus to Radio, checking it over for damage. It had its sleeves pulled down over its fingertips and it had sprouted dark eyebags on skin a couple shades paler than True remembered it being. Everything else hid under layers of loose clothing, but it didn't look like it was bleeding or anything. It watched them back, motionless, waiting.

"Where are we?"

It dropped its gaze, tugging at its sleeves. Great sign. Nerves clawed down their spine. Were those bruises on its neck?

The bathroom door hit the wall with a deafening crack. An impossibly bright man burst in, crossed the room in a single stride. Radio barely picked up its legs in time to miss getting bulldozed by a bolt of lightning in platinum hair and pasty skin.

"My star patient!" The man bellowed, plucking True out of the tub as if they weighed nothing. Their vision flashed white. Lava under the stitches. Hot—frigid—hot.

"Buck up!" the man commanded, holding True upright on their watery legs. Their stomach clenched, shunting bile up and not quite out. Their groan morphed into a gag.

"My my oh manners. My bedside is the best!"

The support vanished and True dropped like a brick. Caught themself on the lip of the grimy tub, but it was about as effective as catching a rock with a square of toilet paper. They screamed over the first half of whatever the man said. He kept blathering through True's sudden and thunderous tinnitus.

"...Doctor Allsaint, fantastic to see you're recovering well!" he told the wall.

Yeah, recovering so well. They spit bitter slime and pressed their cheek to the cool edge of the tub. It helped, a smidge... they pretended it helped. The man—Dr. Allsaint, they assumed— bent at the waist like a reticulated doll. Stiff, plastic in the lifelessness of the motion. His eyes lagged, set deep in scraped-out hollows. They were blue, but the lakes surrounding them stained them darker. And they shook, uncontrollably his eyes shook.

"Get *up*," he said.

True ground their teeth, breathing slow through their nose while their vision swam. They couldn't feel their legs. And they were sure they were making a fatal mistake, not moving quick enough, but they were barely hanging on.

They flexed their fingers, trying to force co-operation from their body. Jammed their arm underneath them for leverage. No luck. Out of the blue, Radio was there, helping them to their feet, pulling their arm over its shoulders. It had to be holding their whole weight because they certainly weren't.

"Good," the doctor all but purred. He drew up their shirt and stuck his nose close to the crooked row of small, tidy stitches. They would have kneed him in the schnozz if they could have. "Lucky you, that bullet only nicked your liver."

Bullet, right. They remembered being shot, remembered Hrōkr, vaguely remembered glimpses of green, fresh air, dizzying motion. Freezing cold.

"Bullet for bullet for bullet for bullet. Ha, fitting. You know, that's a good spot for a kidney surgery." Dr. Allsaint was saying. True squinted at him, struggling to cling to the present.

"What?" they rasped. Dr. Allsaint's expression wavered, sharpened into something less disgustingly cheery.

"You know, you know, you, you." He bit his tongue, dropped their shirt. By the time he straightened he seemed to have regained his train of thought. "You met my darling Eliza before you ever got shot. Smart. Psychic, even. Her bullet, your bullet. Too lucky."

My darling Eliza.

Getting dropped on their nice new bullet wound hadn't woken them up, but that connection certainly did.

"We should go," they said. "Where's my pack?"

Dr. Allsaint paused, looking at them but not really looking. He licked his teeth. For whatever reason, that gesture unnerved True.

"Walking is important for recovery," he said at last, turning to the side in a motion that might have been an invitation to leave, except the room was so small that even sideways he took up all the space between the defunct sink and the mold-speckled wall. He waited politely. Radio's eyes flicked between the two of them, and the three inches of space Allsaint expected them to squeeze through.

"Let's not dilly dally, out you get," Allsaint said.

"Love to," True muttered.

"Great!"

At that, he turned and marched out of the cramped bathroom, ducking to get through the door.

"Buddy's a nutjob," True whispered to Radio as it helped them out of the tub. Their legs were making a slow return to the land of the living. They gripped the sink, stopping to catch their breath. Blink away static. Evaluate. All ten fingers, all nine toes.

Something or someone thumped on the upstairs floor and knocked a spindle-legged beetle out of the rafters. It landed in Radio's hair with an audible plop. True flicked it off, and Radio shuddered.

Time to get out of there.

Wherever there was.

Dismal grey slime seeped from the dismal grey ceiling into spongy fungus-infested walls. A long hall split the house in two, from the front door to a teeming shadowed depth. The swollen walls had grown around a handful of portraits and diplomas. Rusted nails jutted from all the eyes, condensation clouded the glass from the inside, snippets of words peering out.

Allsaint, M.D.

Eliza Schecter, BsN.

Mushrooms shaped like ripples of shelves climbed the hallway walls. Small glass jars teetered precariously on the wider shelves, egg-shaped bulges floating in the cloudy water. True could swear those blobs tracked their hobble toward the decrepit front door. A person-shaped lump shoved in the corner rocked back, forth, bounced off the wall and rocked backwards again.

"Have you been discharged?" Dr. Allsaint's voice reached out of the darkness shrouding the back of the house.

True bit back a groan.

"Yes," they said. The exist was right there, inviting them out, telling them they would be fine if they crossed the threshold. Their gut, however, told them that the swarm behind them was straining at the bit and fully capable of popping their skull off their vertebrae.

"Congratulations on your recovery." Allsaint announced, suddenly much closer. A dweller startled out of the dark, careening down the hall. Radio wrested True out of the way, its grip burrowing in their side.

"Ow," they breathed. A mistake. Radio's death grip softened but not before Allsaint's shivering hand glommed onto True's shoulder.

"If you're in pain you should not leave!" his bellowing was deafening up close. He spun them about. The bullet wound pulled with the motion, shooting fiery gouts up their side. They chomped down on their tongue, swallowing a cry, and forced themself to focus on one of Allsaint's twin swaying faces.

His blond eyebrows knit in seemingly genuine concern. The expression was at odds with all the too-sharp angles of his face, the crooked, healed broken nose, the ghoulishly pale eyes with nothing behind them.

"Let go of me," True demanded, slowly, inhaling very carefully so as not to set off the burning all over again. The hall behind Allsaint writhed with curious shadows. Hungry shadows.

"I'm a doctor, if you show me where it hurts I can help."

"It hurts where you took the fucking bullet out," they bit out. Every fiber of their being screamed to get away. In the next five seconds they were going to nail him in the dick, stitches be damned.

Allsaint let go in snail-paced increments. His face warped around the two dead spots that were his eyes. A poorly molded Claymation of first confusion, then fury, then deeper confusion.

"Ah, I see. I... see," he chewed on his words. True was already scooting out of reach. Radio at their back, half holding them upright, half leading the way.

"Where are you going? It's nearly time for tea." Allsaint sank farther into the confusion, the shadows behind him swelled at the mention of tea. Sharp teeth flashed.

"I don't think so."

"I'm right."

Damn, this dude would not let up. They scraped their fuzzy brain for something, anything, to get them out.

"I can't stay," they started. Come on, think. Think, think. "I told Eliza, I would... not, have tea. Today."

"Eliza!" Allsaint exploded, whirling about with impressive and frightening speed. Some part of him left a dent in the wall with a solid thwack that he didn't acknowledge. "My darling Eliza."

True and Radio ducked out the rotted door before the final, ringing vowel. The hallway shifted, floorboards moaning out a chorus as the shadows surged, suddenly bold. Most bunched around Allsaint. Few snaked into the crevices closer to the door. Reaching, nipping, chasing. A shadow with sharp teeth and a tangle of dark hair stopped in the doorway, grinning at their retreat. Eliza waved, reached out, and slammed the door shut.

"Hurry, before Doctor Crazy jumps out the window," True urged, turning their back on the infested house. Radio folded its arm around his waist again. Onto the cracked street. Into a city much larger than the village they'd been shot in.

15
The Home of the Enemy

The pair reached the end of the desolate street and paused for True to catch their breath. They needed shelter, and desperately wanted their pack.

"Gallows!" a familiar voice startled True for the second time in too few minutes. They bit down a frustrated scream. Craned towards none other than Suni Valdivia, her daughter and two other civilians stood with her.

The barn owl and the feral cat, they realized when they got closer. Linc's bodyguards look a little different in the midday sun, sans the cowering and slinking. All their backs were unburdened, a detail that clenched True's stomach. If Radio didn't have their pack Valdivia didn't have their pack, then they'd just run out of people who might have brought it along to—wherever there was. They couldn't bear the thought of it lost somewhere in the Rockies. It made the inside of their head feel like a hive of angry thought-insects.

"Look who survived." That was Valdivia's version of a greeting. Her voice butted into the haze. "Good damn thing, too, you've got enough of my blood in you."

"Your blood."

"O positive." She tapped her inner elbow, as if that answered a damn thing.

"How the fuck do you know that?" they asked. The smaller Valdivia's head bobbled at her mother's side. "Hell," they corrected themself.

"You remember the house."

Right, the spooky too-clean house with the fridge full of blood bags and the cabinets stuffed with blood-typing kits. They remembered.

Big Valdivia waited a beat for the memory to sink in before she continued. "The factioneers who stayed there had a bunch of old transfusion tools and I used to be a vet. Between the two of us, we got you earthside." She gestured to Radio.

"Earth," they let the word die and unspool bonelessly from the end of a too-short breath. Down by their waist, out of sight, Radio looped the tail of their sash around their hand. Rough fabric scratched their skin. "Where?"

"Vancouver," Valdivia tipped her head in the opposite direction, motioning for them to walk with her. "We're on our way back to my caravan now, come with us."

"Where is my pack?"

"Don't worry, I know how you scavengers are with your stuff. It's safe at my caravan, everything's the same except your first air kit is used up."

The thought insects riled, swarming down their spine. They knew before Valdivia spoke that if the pack had made it here with them, it wouldn't have made it untouched, but knowing it and hearing about it were different. Hearing about it filled them with disquiet that they were too raw to deal with.

Rough fabric tightened over their hand. They pinched a tassel, rolling it between their thumb and finger. The bite of the thread brought them back. Not all the way, but it made them a little less like a hive of angry bees. They hadn't lost everything, they had what was in their pockets, and if they trusted—that was a stretch, alright, *believed* Valdivia, then their pack was waiting for them.

"That's your biggest concern?" The Cal dropped his two cents into the conversation.

"Yeah, Cal, it is," True said, grinding the tassel into the side of their finger. Survival first, details later. If that was the kind of question Cal asked then maybe he was less of a feral cat and more of a house pet.

"You remember." Mu, the owl-faced one, beamed. He scratched the back of his neck, smile melting into a nervous chuckle. Scrunching his fists into the crooks of his elbows, thumbs under fingers. Not much fighting sense in him, True thought. It was a wonder Linc had picked him up as a bodyguard. He was monstrously tall, and without a lick of sense he would be almost too easy to manipulate. A personal golem.

"Did you see her?" Mu sank to a stage whisper, as if it wasn't already difficult to hear him, "in there?"

"Was it scary in there?" Valdivia's mini-me bubbled in. She, too, framed her question in a stage whisper. She turned to peer at True with her good eye, knocking into her mother as she did.

Big Val righted her with a gentle, practiced ease. "I bet it was scary."

"It's not that scary," Mu said.

"To you!" Little Val crossed her arms. "There's shadow monsters in there, they could eat me."

"Eliza's a—"

Big Valdivia cleared her throat, cutting off Mu. His mouth snapped shut, a lick of repentance curling his shoulders up to his ears. But the kid wasn't stupid, and True could see the colour draining from her face.

Speaking of the fox woman.

"Eliza traded something to get me fixed," they cut in, drawing the attention from the nightmarish children-eating shadows. They needed to know how much they had to trade back to make up for the stitches. "Explain that to me."

It was Cal who filled in the blanks. "We didn't know Linc's gun was empty. Eliza put it together after that comment you made."

"She's smart," Mu interrupted.

"She's crazy," Cal said, "she dragged us all up here to hang out with Doctor Demented."

"This is her home," Mu said softly.

Cal started to snap back, but caught himself, grey eyes darting to the kid. "Whatever. We're here now, and since we owed you one for the bullet, so are you. You're welcome." He wrapped up his story the same way he'd started it quick and to the point.

Well, at least that was one question answer.

❧

The Valdivias led them down a coastal road, past a broken-down pier shelter. Patchy slate clouds and dark, choppy waters spanned the distance between where they crouched and the fist-sized island teeming with activity. Rusted metal and greying wood made up the ancient metal monolith, bay doors hung open like a hungry mouth to take in its victims. Gravel and foot traffic kept most of the island foliage at bay, and if True craned they could make out the corner of a storage shed tucked on the other side of the island.

Sheets of pressboard and old tarps had been fastened over the places in the factory walls where the elements had eaten the exterior or windows had been smashed out. Someone had spray painted a fire red medic symbol over on of the boards and it cast an angry gaze over the only way onto the island; a concrete bridge that had been washed away.

Who else was watching? There were two patrols circling the island, and one stationed on the factory side of the bridge, but True couldn't tell if there were any more spying out of the upper levels of the factory itself.

"Used to be a fishing factory," Big Valdivia whispered, "the Reds moved in last summer... come to think of it, we lost a lot of the caravan around that time, too."

"Lost?" True asked.

Big Valdivia shrugged. "There hasn't been an After Market in this area since those guys arrived. We've been forced to go farther for new supplies, and we knew some people left to join the Faction but the rest? We figured they found greener pastures."

Grim silence settled over the group. True tracked a factioneer as he walked across the bridge. They couldn't help but notice how high out of the water the be-barnacled, rotting pillars lofted the main platform. It made their stomach clench. But they'd have to get over it, at least for the minute it would take to get over the bridge. Running a finger over their stitches, they peeled off from the group.

"Where are you going?" Big Valdivia hissed.

"Across that bridge?" they tried. They hadn't planned farther ahead than that.

"And?"

They threw up their hands, winced at the pull to their stitches. And? It was a stupid idea. And? They weren't thinking clearly. They weren't anything clearly, the world filtered to them through bubble wrap and gauze. And? They hadn't come this far to do nothing.

"How are you getting across?" Big Valdivia trailed after them with her hands on her hips, and Radio had abandoned the unspoken shovel's length rule to creep along inside their personal bubble. They nudged it back a couple steps. Personal space was personal space, and they could walk fine on their own now.

"Walking," they said, lifting their feet extra high for emphasis, and also because they were a child, apparently.

"What will you do if you make it to the island?"

Sighing, True stopped and turned to face her. They aimed an imaginary gun at her head.

"Pitches, from the woman holding all my tools captive."

"Come to the caravan for the night. We can make a real plan, rest, eat."

"We," they repeated, rocking back on their heels, they narrowed their eyes at her. Great, good, exactly what they wanted, to be around dozens more people. "Last time I tried to warn people it didn't go well."

"This time you have me," Valdivia countered, "the caravan knows me, and they know something fishy is going on around here, they'll listen."

True wanted to argue that Valdivia herself hadn't been willing to listen when they'd first met. But the truth was, True made people uncomfortable, Valdivia didn't.

"The Faction wasn't your problem two weeks ago. Your words."

"Quit being stubborn."

Bang, they squeezed the imaginary trigger and hobbled away. Stubborn was right. They had come here for one reason, and one reason only, and they would be damned if they didn't get that shit done.

"Wait." Her hand landed on their shoulder, unrelenting as she pulled them off course.

'If I have to light myself on fire to burn the Faction down, I will." They said it and they meant it. Shoving her off, they turned and had to rear back to avoid Cal. Someone really needed to teach these people what a space bubble was.

"Frankly, that's the stupidest thing I've heard in a while," he said and nailed True between the eyes.

A muffled commotion followed. Radio hooked Cal's ankle and snapped his feet from under him. A move that it definitely could have pulled before he'd crunched True's nose. Its grip closed on True's elbow, preventing them from staggering away. Valdivia snagged their other side at the same time and clamped her hand over their mouth. Mu broke Cal's fall, stumbling under his weight with wide eyes. By the time the first drop of True's blood hit the foliage, the dust was settling.

The groans of the swaying bridge swept across the shore, carrying Little Valdivia's quiet, "Mom? Is that Ali?"

"No, honey," Big Valdivia said. Lied. She was a shit liar, True thought, watching her knuckles go bloodless around her staff and her expression crumple and smooth with an effort.

A pair of factioneers cut across the bridge, quick like sharks through calm water. Faction patches decorated their jackets and a flopping red-headed body hooked between them. The redheads feet dragged in the dirt, and blood darkened the fronts of the factioneers' grey shirts.

True wrenched free of Big Valdivia, unsuccessfully. She let go anyway, in favour of cupping her daughter's face to turn her away from the bridge. True pulled their mask down to mop up the blood. Pinch and tilt, except they didn't have much to pinch so they settled for more of a smush and tilt.

"*Tuguy*," they muttered, shooting Cal a nasty glare. Radio smacked them.

"You're fine." Cal said.

"Come over here, I'll teach you how find it feels," True said, a sentiment that was greatly damaged by a wave of vertigo. Reluctantly, they steadied themself on Radio.

The frenetic energy True had been wired with since the fungus house drained out on the river running from their nose. Dizzy and exhausted in a way that made their lungs feel heavy, they managed to keep their legs mostly under them, and that was it.

The factioneers hurried North, away from the group hiding in the bushes. Smearing the last slug of blood from their nose, True pulled their mask into place and crept after the factioneers. Instinct told them to run the other way, but there was a hole in their gut where all their common sense was falling out. Or something like that. Their thoughts unravelled. Which meant they didn't have long to find out what those two factioneers were up to with poor Ali.

Radio pinched their coat. Valdivia might have been distracted, but it wasn't, and neither were Cal and Mu.

"Do you want to know what the Faction is doing here or not?" True whispered, breaking free of Radio's loose grip. Radio crossed its arms, but followed instead of stopping them.

"Wait."

They waited. More out of fear of getting whacked with that big stick Valdivia carried than anything. The factioneers shrank into the treeline, the opportunity to follow shrinking with them.

"Mu, come with me back to the caravan," Big Valdivia beckoned to him. She had her daughter tucked protectively under her arm, and she held out her hand. When the sunlight pooled in her calloused palm and the creases around her eyes, she looked downright motherly. For an instant, True could see a glimmer of who she would have been, before.

Too bad the apocalypse had scraped the kindness out of people a long time ago. She just wanted a big body to scare off lurkers while she walked back to her stay.

Mu cast a nervous glance to Cal, his thumbs dug little white tracks into the corners of his elbows. Only after Cal gave an approving nod did he split from Cal's side and join the Valdivias.

Alright, now that that was settled.

The factioneers had disappearing into the treeline opposite the shelter. True wasted no time scuttling across the clearing. They had to hope the watchdog on the other side of the bridge would pass them off as a passing wanderer. In a matter of seconds, they were creeping into the brush again, with Cal and Radio trailing behind, the factioneers' heads bobbing in their vision.

Deeper into the buckled city they limped, the gravel under their feet turning into broken concrete. With the sun beating down on them and grass tickling the tops of their palms. The blood damping their mask kept the pollen at bay, for now.

A handful of caved-in car frames dotted the street, unsteady tall buildings swayed on either side. A desire path had been trampled into the brush, drag marks and browning blood decorating the crushed foliage. The factioneers lurked between rusted car frames in a sheltered parking lot, stopping in a slab of sunlight that poured from a hole in the concrete above. One turned to the other, said something that made them both laugh, and they dropped the body.

Anger sparked over True's too-warm skin. That was it? They were leaving him there? The Red Faction had the gall to call scavengers immoral and degenerate and *that* was how they treated the dead?

They didn't even notice the factioneers turning to come back down the desire path until Cal grabbed them and dragged them into a bush-crowded alley. Heart cramping their throat, they peered through the dense branches. Spots danced in their vision, and they could hear the chatter and footfall of the approaching factioneers.

They reached for their shovel. Shit, it was with their pack. They grabbed a broken concrete chunk instead, clicking through the math in their head. Two factioneers, three of them. Cal could throw a punch and Radio gripped its knife under its poncho.

Sucking in air, they held their breath as the chatter grew close. Radio's arm snaked out, its fingers dug into the back of

True's neck, sticking them in place until the factioneers passed by.

As soon as the chatter had faded out of earshot, True shoved it into the wall. It flicked both hands away from its eyes and pointed at them, a reproachful scowl on its face.

"I don't know what that means but when I figure it out I'm gonna kick your ass," True said, straggling to their feet. They stumbled towards the patch of sunlight. Someone had to take care of that corpse and the Faction sure as hell wasn't going to.

"I'm surprised you two are still traveling together. Shadow crawlers and scavengers don't normally get along."

"It's a scavenger."

"A scavenger without a pack," Cal said like he thought it was bullshit. Because it was bullshit.

"Yeah." True snapped back. They weren't in the mood. "And why would you care." He was the one who came all the way out here with Eliza, and she was the one with filed teeth.

"I don't, but Suni won't like it, and neither will the caravan."

True walked a little faster in hopes of leaving the conversation behind. Cal was right, but their head hurt too much to think out a solution right then.

The soft hush of grass and crickets blanketed the parking lot. A body lay akimbo in the sunlight, painfully bright hair matched a gaping red slash across his throat, purple-black bruises ringed his raw wrists and ankles. And he wasn't the only one.

Row after row of corpses heaped into little piles littered the parking lot. None stacked higher than the wild grass, so that from a distance the grass and the car skeletons obscured them. All a bloodless grey, stained with matching bruises and withered by the elements. And most of them... True touched the edge of their mask.

"Oh, fuck." Cal's strained voice came from very far away.

The body of the redhead marked the start of a new pile. His brown eyes had frozen open, and blank, one tiny and mucus-y.

If anybody asked, they would argue that the weakness in their watery knees came from the injury, a remnant of the pipe cleaner legs. Never mind the sinking in their chest, the weird old sore spot behind their solar plexus. All consequences of being overtired. They did not feel for the half-blind corpse, did not wonder whether the body would have been theirs, or Radio's.

They did not feel.

With practiced hands they straightened out the body, drew out their lighter, flicked it once. Twice. The tiny yellow flame swayed peacefully, ready to scorch away the evils soaking into the parking lot earth. With a grimace, they buried it back in their pocket. If they couldn't march straight across that bridge from here, then they couldn't afford to let the Faction know they were here, yet.

They found Radio standing over a heap, tracing the bruise that ringed its neck. The pattern stamped into its skin matched the marks on the corpses. It watched them out of the corner of its eyes, its lips compressed into a flat line. They signed its name.

Lifting its hands, it hesitated, then seemed to think twice about signing and crouched to write in the dirt instead.

Back later.

And it walked away.

16
The Cauliflower Head

Woozy, dry-mouthed, and in general, grouchy. True sat under a patch of northern lights the shimmered through a broken ceiling. Big Valdivia's caravan was camped in an old warehouse, uncomfortably close to the docks. Fires sprinkled the concrete floor, tended by the more nocturnal caravan travellers. The fires shed warmth and cozy light into the cool night combatting the cold concrete that sapped True's body heat. It was almost kind of comfortable, except for the dull throb in their side, and all the people.

Radio had yet to return. They regretted not wandering off with it. There were too many people here who stared at True too long out of the corners of their eyes. At least they had their pack back. They held it in their lap, they had waited for the caravan civilians to drift off to bed to shield the process of examining its eviscerated innards from prying eyes. It felt unbalanced in their hands, they would have known someone had dug around in it, even if Suni hadn't admitted to it.

Biting down the ripple of discomfort with a reminder that they'd left Valdivia with no choice, they unsnapped the top of the pack. The handgun winked at them from on top of everything else they owned. They popped the magazine, eyeballed it. One bullet of the five they had started with remained. If they held still, they could feel the ghost of the kickback buzzing the spaces between their joints. Tight, pressurized vibrations. Different from the resounding clang that came with striking with their shovel.

Clicking the magazine back into place, they zipped the gun into a side pocket. In reach but not staining the rest of their things with its oil.

With the efficiency of familiarity, they emptied the rest of the pack. Inventories. Tucked everything into its proper spot.

All stuff accounted for, except food. And the salve. There would be a market here tomorrow though. Albeit a regular market, not an After Market but there were bound to be a few merchants who were willing to deal with a scavenger.

Laying their head on their pack a final out-of-place lump prodded them. They reached up and dug it out of the shallow topmost pocket. It came with a crinkle, ancient newspaper folded neatly around a hard object.

A flat tin fell loose of the paper wrapping and smacked onto their forehead, writing on the lid. An annoyed grimace painted their face, they twisted it open, peering in at what appeared to be a balm. A tiny purple flower had been pressed into the cream surface, reminiscent of the flowers Radio had fastened to its poncho.

That did not belong in their pack.

They resealed the tin and tilted it to catch the light of the fire and reveal the words scratched onto the lid.

Balm: self-heal flower, tallow. Cuts, scrapes, bruises.

They recognized Radio's writing from the sand and narrowed their eyes at it. They would ask Radio about it, whenever it poked its head up again.

As if summoned by their thoughts, Radio's shape blotted out the shifting green lights over their head. It wobbled there, as if watching them, then shuffled off. True propped themself up on an elbow to watch it but it didn't go far. Crunching down in a tight little ball right on the border between one shovel-length away, and the edge of the ring of light cast by the nearest fire. It ignored True, and True was inclined to ignore it, too, in favour of going to sleep. Or brooding some more. Until a glimmer of firelight caught the damp tracks on its cheeks.

Well, shit, that looked like a problem.

They sat up slow, in part not to startle it and in part because, ow.

"Where are you hurt?" they whispered, narrowing their eyes at the lump of black rags as if they'd be able to infrared-vision through the dark and the fabric. Radio shook its head, scrubbing its face.

"Bull," True said. What were they gonna need? Stitches they could manage, dental floss would work fine. But they were out of bandages, bandage substitute, any of that.

Hissing, Radio crooked its pointer fingers at its neck, tilting its head back to show a sliver of throat skin. Green-yellow chain marks ringed the delicate skin there. It touched one, and a shudder went through it. Conveniently, True had a fresh pot of self-heal for that. Scooting closer, they held out the open tin to show Radio.

They'd dipped a finger in before it had a chance to finish shaking its head.

"I'll be gentle," they grumped, dabbing a blob on the first mark. Radio flinched, hard. It caught True's hand in a death grip and hid behind the moth-eaten curtain of its poncho.

"Cut that out," they scolded. They'd seen it walk off a bone-crunching body slam, and this was where it drew the line?

After a long pause, it loosened its grasp. Without the tension of its death grip holding its muscles taut, it began to tremble.

True bit their tongue, gave Radio a second, closer look. They couldn't make out much under the bunches of loose fabric and dancing shadows. Lifting the curtain, they caught it drawing its thumb over the tight, compressed line of its lips again and again, a bloodless afterimage chasing the path like a comet tail. The fire reflected off its glassy, distant eyes.

Not the bruises. Different kind of hurt. One True wasn't so good with. Hesitantly, they put an arm around it, felt it shivering. It's heart thrumming. They couldn't think of any comforting words, so they didn't try to speak, just held on for a while.

Eventually, the shivering calmed, and Radio began to droop face-first towards the floor. Rolling their eyes, True tugged it—gently, so it didn't wake up—to lean on them.

Dumb, now how were they supposed to sleep?

They woke up in the grey of the early morning with Radio's hair imprinted on their cheek. Radio snored quietly, sound asleep. And True's bladder demanded to be relieved *right now*. Ugh. At least that meant things were working in there, right?

Easing Radio to the ground, they snuck away to find a private hole in the dirt. Outside, birds trilled annoying ditties to see who could pester the sun over the horizon. A crude rain-damaged sign cordoned off the designated toilet area. Tall nettles had taken over the outer warehouse walls and provided decent cover to do business. A civilian lurked at the corner of the building, half-hidden by the greenery.

True moved away but kept an eye on the lank grey-streaked back of the civilian's head. Did they know civilians who came out as far as Vancouver? Probably. They tried to work out the math but it fried their tired brain.

They finished up and slipped back inside. Daylight creeped ever closer, brightening the crumbled warehouse. A patch of weak almost-light from the broken ceiling shone on an empty square of concrete. They slowed, gaze flickering over the sleeping civilians. Glanced up at the abandoned rafters. Radio was gone.

It could have been nothing. Radio could have woken up, retreated to somewhere quieter, gone to relieve itself like they had, gone in search of them. There were a hundred reasonable, normal answers for the empty spot.

So, why did their stomach feel like a sinking anchor?

Biting a line into the soft inside of their cheek, they found their answer on a closer sweep of the patch. Their bag had been disrupted. A corner of the threadbare inner lining of the side pocket poked out the zipper. Their heart lurched up to meet their thyroid. They grabbed the first fire watch within reach.

"The person I was sleeping with, where did it go?" They regretted their phrasing as it left their mouth. Regretted it more when the fire watch cocked an eyebrow at them.

"Get your mind out of the gutter," they grumbled, already dropping the fire watch in favour of scanning the warehouse floor. Sleeping lumps, the beginning stretches of the market, and Big Valdivia with her staff. But no Radio.

Valdivia waved. Cal with her as they strode in True's direction.

"I know who you mean, they went of with the new guy," the fire watch said, pointing, and True took off. Winding as fast as they could around the sleeping bodies. They heard Valdivia call their name and ignored her, ducking through a gap in the warehouse wall.

Nettles, trampled grass, a chain link fence with no links left. And there, at the end of the street; Radio, Jonesy, and Galya's gun in the narrow space between them. That greasy thieving snake.

"Gallows!" Big Valdivia spoiled whatever element of surprise True might have had. As their name rang out over the cool morning mist, Jonesy's mock-gentle mouth tensed into a gritted frown. He goaded Radio into a run, dragging it behind a long overgrown fence. True bolted after them. Big Valdivia made quick time stepping in front of them, Cal stuck on her tail.

"Wait, now," she started to say.

"He took Radio," they said. Jonesy didn't have that much of a head start, and they were pretty sure of his destination. The ocean cast up a salty breeze, a thin sliver of the water visible from the end of a long stretch of street corners, collapsing fences, and shipping yards butted up on the backs of each other. They had a straight shot from here to the water's edge. If only Valdivia would get her hand off their shoulder.

They knocked her away, right in time to hear her say, "it's a shadow dweller."

Damn.

Recoil took them out of her reach. Her arm lingered in the dead air they left. They saw her gears turning, the edge of her lip indented where she bit the inner corner. She saw them, too, the hard set of their eyes over the mask Radio Silent had given them.

"You knew." Disappointment dripped off her quiet accusation. Valdivia's knuckles creaked around her staff, the indent at the corner of her mouth flattening. "That thing isn't your friend, it's a dangerous cannibal."

"Thing," they snorted, a sharp stab in their side buried under a hot rush of rage. They shoved past her, and Cal shifted out of their path, perturbed feral cat energy bunched in his shoulders.

"Fuck—Gallows—you can't come back here with a dweller," Valdivia shouted at them. They tossed a fast, loose middle finger in her direction and veered oceanward, sweat dripping onto their tongue. Shit, getting shot had crushed their stamina.

A thin haze of rain had coated everything in the time it took True to spill out on the ocean end of the frantic yard sprint. Sweating, shivering, their side a crater of magma. A reedy body squeezed through the broken boards of the last fence. Coming back, not running away. Jonesy lurched when he spied True, clothes snagging on the splintered wood.

True ripped him from the hole by his grimy shirt collar, knee finding the old injury on his leg. He yelped, eyes bulging.

Crack.

Jonesy's teeth left dents on their knuckles.

Red, red, red. There really was something to that old saying, *seeing red.* Jonesy, dirt. The thud of a body hitting packed earth. True drove him down, knee right up with his chin and shin following the length of his breastbone. He sputtered and gasped. Hands empty of the gun and Radio nowhere to be seen. True reeled back in search of a second body. The pull lit every one of their stitches on fire and they bit their tongue hard to keep a scream down.

They heaved forward again. Steel toe *gently* pushing Jonesy's groany, writhing body into the dirt. He squeaked like a spent toy.

They crouched low, too close to Jonesy's tomato face. What remained of their nose crinkled in disgust as his panicked breathing skittered over them, slimy, just like the rest of him.

They pulled their mask down, giving him full view of their scar because they knew, for all his kindness, their face horrified him.

"Once chance, Jonesy."

His swelling red eyes tracked toward the ocean. At a second glance, they caught what they'd missed before; they were right back at the pier.

There was Otsana.

There was Radio.

There was a knife.

All swaying on the world's worst tightrope. True left a crack in Jonesy's ribcage and scrambled out the fence. They stopped to pry a rotted board free, rusted nails jutted from the end. An impromptu weapon, since they'd left their shovel with their pack.

Sagged on one of the foremost bridge legs was a putrid lump that True had mistaken for a split garbage bag, it hadn't been there yesterday, and it wasn't until they were almost on top of it that they recognized the stumps sticking out from the lower half as feet.

A decrepit corpse swayed in the fog, lashed upright to the bridge. From the knees down it looked like a savage animal had used its legs as chew toys, stripping away clothing and flesh until what remained were lumps of pink and white and greasy grey-green. A fat white maggot squirmed out of a hole in the wet membranous sole of a foot that had been scraped down to muscle and tendon. It hit the ground and burst like a boil under True's boot. Blood, black with age, clumped over the stumpy cauliflower remains of the head, and the skin that showed through its torn clothes was purple with bloat.

Otsana had lost her fucking mind.

A dozen too-short too-long strides and they set foot on the bridge, felt the damp wood give and their stomach hit the dirt. Funny, they hadn't realized it could drop any lower than it already had. The bridge groaned and listed leftward, and every molecule in their body froze. Their feet stuck like pikes had been driven through them into the planks.

"Scared?" Otsana jeered, voice sharp and jagged. If they'd looked up at her they would have seen hatred curling her lip, lighting her obsidian eyes like chips of still-hot volcanic rock. She was nothing but hate and hurt bound in basalt skin. There was nothing she would not have done to scorch them.

But they weren't watching her, they were watching Radio. Its wrists and elbows had been winched together with zip ties, but it jabbed its fingers, trying to sign.

Otsana's knife curved a hair, drawing a thin line of blood from Radio's throat. Radio winced, pulling the knife farther across its skin.

"Don't." The plea jolted out of them, perhaps surprising True more than anyone else.

Otsana's laugh set their hair on end. "I hope you suffer like I do." She sliced the knife into Radio.

The next second stretched into a dozen. Every muscle, every ligament in the hand that held the knife tightened. Blood spilled over the blade.

True smashed the steel toe of their shoe into the bridge support, shaking the corpse and sending a shudder through the planks. The bridge swayed, shifting Otsana's balance just so, for an instant. Seizing the sliver of chance, Radio slammed its head into her face.

The Radio-Otsana tangle stumbled on the damp planks. Otsana clinging to Radio, clawing for a better grip while her weight pitched them both too hard whichever way she tilted, ruining their traction. It slipped. True lurched onto the bridge, petrifying fear of heights abandoned for a fleeting instant.

With a sharp jab and a surprised grunt from Otsana, Radio broke free. Eyes wide, it threw its arms up, reaching. No, pointing. It should have kicked Otsana, it should have turned so it could see her coming. True grabbed its outstretched arms to pull it from her, but her blade vanished between folds of black cloth.

True had known Radio could laugh.

Now they knew Radio could scream.

17
The Swaying Bridge

Boot met flesh with a crunch that sent Otsana scraping to the splintered bridge ledge. Radio crumpled, skull striking the planks.

True's boot came down on the other side of Radio's limp body. Guarding it. Their nail-studded fence plank levelled at Otsana while she crawled back to her feet. Both—empty—hands flat on the splintered wood. Fuck, where was the knife?

They chanced a look down. Found it. Laying in a pool of ruby red beside Radio, blood seeped onto the grey wood.

Otsana grinned as the bridge swayed and sent a tremor through True. Her glassy eyes tracked the waver of their makeshift weapon.

Frigid metal dented the bare skin of their neck and Jonesy's heavy breathing skirted their cold ears.

Stupid, stupid, stupid. How could they have forgotten that gun?

Gravel crunched behind them, some factioneer coming back from the death pit parking garage that Otsana clearly ached to send them to.

"What are you going to do now?" Otsana asked.

"Bite me." Their voice was impossibly tight. Choppy waves smacked the legs of the bridge, grey sky reflected on greyer waters. Sweat and rain dripped down their spine, leaving chills in their wake. Radio was too, too still beneath them.

Get up, Radio, get up.

The gravel crunching ended with an abrupt thud and a gut-deep loss of air from Jonesy. The pressure vanished from True's neck.

"I'll tell you what you're gonna do," Cal said, a faint twang in his voice that True had never noticed before. "You're gonna back up." He punctuated his instruction with the click of a safety. The muzzle of a gun, held steady, preceded him past True.

Reluctantly, Otsana inched backwards.

The instant Cal was between them and Otsana, True dropped. Throwing the plank of the bridge, their hands found Radio. One to the stab wound, staunching the blood. One sliding under its neck and shoulder. Cold, scarred skin against trembling fingertips. They lifted it to press their ear to its chest.

"Please, Radio," they whispered, the patter of rain drowning out their plea, "please, please, please."

A heartbeat, weak and slow. Calloused fingers wrapped around their wrist, Radio's eyes screwed open, sharp with pain. It curled around its injury, like a black hole had opened in its ribcage to suck it into oblivion.

"How we going back there, True?" Cal asked.

"We're fine, we're fine." They weren't sure if they repeated it to convince him, or themself. It wasn't working either way. They had to stop this bleeding, they had to get off this bridge. They pressed the injury harder. Hot blood poured between their fingers, the only warm thing about Radio.

Cal glanced at them, mouth curved downwards. Turning back to Otsana, he motioned with the handgun. "Go on now, go hide in your hole," he said.

"That thing isn't even loaded," Otsana snarled, moving neither towards them nor away. Without missing a beat, Cal tightened his trigger finger.

"You wanna find out? Ain't wasting a bullet on a warning shot."

True scooped Radio's limp, wet body into their arms and retreated to the safety of the solid ground.

Slowly, slowly, Otsana's hand came up in mock surrender and she walked backwards to the safety of the other factioneers at the end of the bridge. The commotion had drawn a curious crowd, but the threat of gunfire held them back. Distance and rain turned Otsana into a blur looming under the rusted arch of the fishery doors. True could feel her glare burning holes into them.

Cal waited for her to disappear beyond the weathered fishery wall before shoving the gun into his waistband.

"Come on," he said, taking True by the shoulders, "before she comes back with friends."

They escaped as far as the treeline and put the largest closest tree between them and the fishery. They scrambled through their pockets for something to help. Fishing line, a spork, old pen, half a set of rusty lock picks, lighter. The bottle of azithro pills rattled as it hit the ground. Those were only going to be useful if Radio lived to get an infection. They shoved the pills back in their pocket and grabbed the lighter. Sparked it, held it to the zip ties until the plastic snapped, then put the flame to the metal handle of the spork.

Radio caught on, peeling layers and rolling up the hem of its blood-soaked shirt. Red painted skin and scar all the same shade, the knife had left a ragged tear, half a finger length long and hemorrhaging.

"Are you sure that's a good idea?" Cal asked, crouching to get a better look at the injury. "Look where it is, if that's as deep as it looks—"

"I know!" True snapped. "Deep breath," they told Radio, then pressed the white-hot handle to the injury.

It gasped, writhed. Face contorting in a silent scream. And True pressed the hissing instrument harder into its wound, grateful that they couldn't smell the burning flesh. Its foot pistoned into their shin and knocked them on their ass. The spork bounced off a tree root and into the underbrush to sizzle unhappily, a neon angry mark blistered on Radio's ribcage.

"Gonna live?" True asked.

It flopped its head back against the tree, drawn and exhausted and shivering, and pushed the back of its hand outward.

"You look really alive for a dead person."

It flipped them the bird.

At least it was alive enough to do that.

Hauling themself to their feet, True offered their hand to Radio. The sooner they put distance between them and the fishery, the better.

It hadn't recovered the body heat it had dumped out on the bridge, but it managed to get its legs under it. Wavering while it gripped their hand through a wave of something that blanched all the blood from its face.

They made it out of the woods, down the street. Slow, but steady. Fog rolled in off the unsettled ocean to nip at their heels. Radio listed and stumbled into them, its eyelids drooped down to the sidewalk. Its weight made their muscles shake. True doused their worry in all the annoyance they could muster.

A week ago, carrying Radio would have been nothing. They didn't even have their pack weighing them down.

A week ago, they hadn't been shot.

Whatever, they just had to make it to the caravan and then they could both sit.

Their dreams of rest evaporated when Valdivia appeared at the head of the last street, staff in hand. With their pack trapped in the warehouse, they needed back in that caravan, with

Valdivia's permission or without it. And Radio was staying with them.

It just sucked that it was ramping up to be a fight.

Two silhouettes prowled half a block behind her. Between brain fog and real fog, True almost mistook the shapes for back-up. Except one was mini-sized and the other towered.

"Mu, buddy, what are you doing out here?" Cal breezed past them. Valdivia glanced over her shoulder, then pivoted a hell of a lot faster, the butt of her staff smacking on the road.

Huh, guess she hadn't known those two were back there.

Gravel scraped behind True, a pebble bounced off their calf.

"Damn it," they hissed out a groan that they felt all the way down in their toes.

A horde of factioneers peaked the hill up the street. Okay, fine, maybe it wasn't a horde, but it was three people too many hellbent on True and Radio.

True cast about for a weapon. Something to pry from the neglected buildings. They should have held on to o that nail board, but they'd needed both hands for Radio. A broken basement window called to them. That would have to do. Propping Radio on the wall, they crouched by the window and tore a strip from their dirty shirt to wrap around the end of a jagged glass shard to wield it like a knife. It wouldn't last long but it would have to do until they got to their pack.

A body plowed into them. Broken glass crunched under them. Swiping blindly with the shard, they caught themself on the window seal. Dust and broken window shards showered on the basement floor below. Great thing to land on. The factioneer pried True's hand from the frame. They jabbed, shard struck torso and stuck. Then snapped, useless. Just their luck, the asshole wore a leather vest.

Radio slashed a knife across his neck. Another strip of leather fell from him. Of course he'd thought to protect his throat. At least someone in this apocalypse had a brain. Too bad it belonged to the enemy.

True kicked hard, snapping the factioneer's legs out from under him before he could take advantage of not being dead. Radio recovered quick, veering to chase the man's descent. Its knife flipped in the air, its eyes bright and sharp. The factioneer hit the gravel. Radio buried the knife in his bared throat.

Blood sprayed, foamy red bubbles forming at the gap where hilt met flesh. Whole body heaving, on its knees, Radio curled over to catch its breath. It wiped at the sweat and blood spatter soaking it forehead while True extricated themself from the shattered window.

"Have you had that knife the whole time?" they asked, brushing glass from their hair. Sea salt and sweat stung in their eyes.

In answer, Radio plucked the knife from the factioneer's throat, wiped the gore off, and slit it into a sheath around its ankle.

"And you didn't gut Jonesy with it?" Irritation set an edge to their tone. Shaking its head, Radio aimed an imaginary gun at its head, the jabbed its thumb at True. Speaking of guns, they grabbed a new glass shard from the debris. It hadn't worked too well last time, but their options had expanded either. One factioneer down, two to go.

A shrill cry and a shout rent the street. True turned to face Cal, scraping himself off the ground with a squashed-bug-splatter bloodstain beneath him, the broken bottom half of a fire escape ladder tangled over his ankles. A second factioneer wrestled Little Valdivia up the shuddering fire escape. The third factioneer fended Big Valdivia off, dancing around her with a metal bat, sneaking blows in on the tail end of her swiping staff.

Radio lurched to its feet, a strange look washed over its face. It blinked fast, lips compressed. Dipping its head, it pressed a hand hard to its chest.

"Listen, I have to get my pack, but you don't owe these people, you don't owe me, and your hurt." True said.

It gripped their shoulder and jabbed at the building next to the one Little Val was being dragged up, at the fire escape. The narrow gap between the two buildings was wall within jumping distance. Radio gave them an insistent shake. Great, they were playing rescuer for other people's kids again.

Ivy vines and tall nettles padded the brick walls and looped around the rungs of a ladder that had seen better days, maybe twenty years ago.

The kid screamed. True snapped toward the sound. Vertigo shoved them a few extra steps to the left. They caught themself on the wall exhaling through a wave of seething ache. Oh, that did not feel good.

They seized a rung and hauled themself up. A second heart pulsed under their gunshot wound While they climbed, the fight between Big Val and the factioneer ended with an abrupt crack. The ladder groaned. A rust-laden rung snapped. True's chin smacked the fire-escape grate. Cursing, the scrambled onto the ledge and squeezed their eyes shut. Tried not to notice how long it took for the metal rung to clang off the concrete.

Little Val's sobs came from far above, and True threw themself recklessly upwards. Up to the roof. Don't think, just make the leap.

A gunshot shattered the air.

They hit the other roof skidding and rolled to a stop on their hands and knees. The factioneer wavered, Little Val nowhere to be seen and True could taste iron in the air. They put their head down and barrelled into the factioneer, flinging her wobbling body off the ledge.

The factioneer hit the concrete the same time that True's knees cracked the ledge, their fingers grasping the roof as they teetered hard. Their throat spasmed shut as they rocked back onto solid ground. A million miles below, Big Valdivia peered up at them from the trigger end of a familiar handgun.

There went their last bullet.

Forcing air past clenched teeth, they reached down and heaved Little Valdivia from the ricket ancient fire escape onto the ledge. They had to work fast, there was no gas left in their tank and they were about one too-long glance down away from turning into a pile of jelly and joining that dead factioneer on the blacktop. None too gently they got the kid onto stable ground and guided her to a jutting pile of air intakes where Little Valdivia mostly sobbed, and True mostly sat with their face buried in their arm and did not think about how they were perched on an ancient-ass falling apart lump of brick held up by expired hopes and wishes.

Big Valdivia and Mu retrieved the two of them, eventually.

A purpling welt stretch from the corner of Big Valdivia's eye into her hairline, she bundled her mini-me into her arms in a flurry of touching and squeezing and a hundred soothing parental murmurs. True slid from the scene and wobbled away.

They paused at the crumpled body of the fallen factioneer. Nudged her onto her back. Crouching, they flitted their hands over her wrists and neck and ears. Into pockets. She'd landed on her face and smashed her teeth in, so they forewent checking in the mouth. They came up empty-handed. Not even a broken watch.

Only old habit had driven them to check in the first place. They couldn't help but go through the motions that had kept them alive for years. And an odd calm came with falling back into a familiar pattern. A dance they knew all the steps to, in the midst of an otherwise hectic disco.

Next step: dig the grave.

A wash of lightheadedness fell through them. After they were done here they were going to crash for a good long time.

That building with the broken window would be an okay place to hole up for a couple hours. It was a little close to this disaster zone, but they were a lot ready to sit. Their side felt like a volcanic cave-in. They had half a mind to give Radio a shake for sending them up that deathtrap ladder.

Wheezing dragged them out of the haze. They looked up to see Radio its lips blue under a sheen of sweat. It clawed at its chest as it hobbled toward them.

Something was wrong.

Its legs buckled beneath it. True lurched to catch it before it cracked its head on the ground.

It hit them with a thud, all its weight at once. Its chest rose and fell too quick, too shallow, too wrong. Suffocating in front of them. It grappled at their coat, clumsy fingers dipping into one of the pockets.

"What do you need?" they asked, skimming the street up and down, as if looking would make medical supplies or their pack magically appear. All they spotted were Cal and Mu, making their way towards True. Even the dead medic at their feet didn't have anything useful.

It scraped the old pen out of their pocket and hit their chest.

Air, it needed air.

They sprang to action. Snapping the top off the pen, they emptied its content out into the fog as fast as they could with numb fingers.

Radio pulled its knife from its ankle sheath, fingers slipping on the handle. It plunged the blade into its own chest and jammed the pen tub into the freshly re-opened stab would. Blood spurted from the tube, hitting Cal square. He reeled back, sputtering. Radio gasped a single full breath, and collapsed, unconscious.

True's hand flew to the pen, holding it steady. Deep red blood drooled out the end of the makeshift chest tube. It needed a doctor, a doctor willing to help a shadow dweller, and the only doctor in this city who would do that listened to exactly one person. Throwing a look to Cal, they said, "Take me to Eliza."

Cal's hesitation lasted a thousand years, and they wanted to scream. Radio Silent was dying. Wiping the blood from his cheek, he gave a curt nod.

"Mu, Suni needs help with the kid."

Their head was full of nothing but panic panic panic.

"But—"

Cal cut him off with a wave. "I can't be everywhere at once. Go."

Taking some of Radio's dead weight, he aimed them back the way they had come and started walking.

In the back of their mind, a little thought-insect crowed that they were going to be paying back the trade to come for the rest of their life, but all they could bring themself to care about was Radio's blood warming their cold fingers.

18
The Fungus House

Gloom shrouded the dilapidated house. The spongy foundations revelled in the fog, mushrooms pushed out of its cracks and corners in search of more to sate their thirst.

Cal knocked on the door, a hand on Linc's old empty gun. True stood at the bottom of the sagging stoop. Their arms full holding Radio. It had woken up with the start of the rain, twelve blocks ago. If you counted delirium as being awake. Every bump and stretch jostled the pen, every breath came as a rattle. Red stained their arms.

"Eliza! We know you're in there," Cal called, banging on the door. His fist struck a soft patch and sank. He pulled free with a squelch, as if the house was reluctant to give up its snack.

"Try Allsaint," True suggested. Allsaint was the one they needed anyways.

Another knock. "Allsaint, is there an Allsaint in—there."

The door sloughed opened between one word and the next, revealed a soggy hall of splinter teeth and tongue-y mushrooms. Screeches ribboned from deep within and curled about Eliza's bird's nest hair.

"Callie," she cooed, throwing her arms all the way about him, so her wrists crossed limp at the back of his neck and her elbows poked out from the apexes of his ears.

"Don't call me that."

She was already flinging apart and sauntering past him, sunken eyes glued to the blood on True's hands.

"Tasty."

"Not one finger."

Eliza's long dirty fingernails skimmed their brow, and she poked one finger to their damp forehead.

"I know why you're here, sunshine, I heard the hollering." She crooked the finger, hooking them inside.

The door squelched shut, the cloudy jars sloshed with the rattle, the things inside them drifting lazily. Hands reached out of the shadows, to pinch pieces off the intruders, growling. True growled right back. If it were possible to hold Radio any closer they did.

"Doctor!" Eliza sang. She kicked open a door that had been kicked open so many times there was a scoop of paint and wood missing from the bottom corner. A pit opened up before her and she descended into it, crooking her finger for them to follow. As if they had any other options. Cal gagged, recoiling.

"Hell, Liza, you live here?"

"Correct."

"You know you could stay with me and Mu. This place is a level four biohazard."

Eliza slowed to a stop, mid-staircase, turning to stare vacuously at Cal. Sallow light painted her waxy, the dark smears under her eyes stretched towards the middles of her hollow cheeks.

"I love it when you talk all nerdy, Callie." She turned back and sank into the pit. And reaching out of the depths to swallow her, Cal, True, Radio; the specter of the good Doctor Allsaint. He jerked up a stair, a doll with stiff, plastic joints.

"Guests, my darling!" he beamed.

"Yes, doctor." Eliza coiled about the doctor, drawing him back into the basement. "Guests who need something."

Doctor Allsaint's lips peeled too far apart, stilting unevenly over the lower half of his face. "Ah! I'm afraid we can't afford any pro bono surgeries today. This economy. You understand."

True pressed their lips together, hurrying down the staircase. No freebies. And here they were without their pack. They got the feeling the shadow dwellers wouldn't want something as simple as earrings.

A crash followed by the hiss of a match sparked a chain reaction of small lights. Dozens of kerosene lamps and stubby candles shone on what appeared to be a massacred pool table. Felt scraped away, nets missing from the cups, and most of the finished had been scratched into oblivion.

The feeling of eyes on them creeped over True's skin. They checked over their shoulder, willing themself not to shudder.

"Recognize it?" Eliza asked, mistaking her wariness.

"Should I?"

She lolled her wrists with a noncommittal hum and slapped the center of the table. They tried to set Radio there carefully, but it moaned, voice brittle and airy from disuse. Eliza's eyebrow arched.

True crushed a snarky remark between their molars. "It's dying, help it."

A smirk flickered over Eliza's vulpine face. "Help it die?"

They were mid-lunge when a pair of spidery hands wrested them back.

"Ah ah," Dr. Allsaint chided. "There is the matter of payment, first."

"What do you want?" True demanded.

"Have a seat." The sharp edge of a chair struck the back of their knees, cutting their feet out from under hem. Eliza's iron grip clamped down on them and Allsaint held up a shaking finger to cut them off before they even opened their mouth.

Bending over Radio, he hummed and hawed. Prodded at the pen chest tube, eliciting another cry from Radio that had True halfway out of the chair before Eliza's unforgiving hold snapped them back onto the hard wood. Allsaint carried on as if the commotion was taking place on another planet and not six inches from him. Scissors had appeared in his hand, possibly from another dimension since True had yet to take their hawkish glare off him and hadn't seen him reach for anything.

Two quick snips parted blood-soaked fabric from hem to pen, Allsaint pulled the poncho back, baring Radio's scars, and frowned at the injury.

"Lucky, lucky," he murmured.

Yeah, getting stabbed was so lucky.

"See this, darling Eliza, this patient should have bled out, but all this scar tissue has restricted the blood flow. Alas, this thingy seems to have hit a lung—oh, there they go."

On the table, Radio had gone boneless.

"Do something!" True struggled against Eliza's hold. Unconcerned, the doctor turned to eye True with infuriating calm.

"You can have whatever you want." Great, now they were begging. Pride swallowed. They should have known better than to let Radio get near them, now they could never go back to how they were before. They could not go back to the loneliness. Radio had to survive, or else True wouldn't.

"You have lovely eyes."

Cold dread sickened True even as they said, "take them."

They choked on panic, fingernails bit into the wood seat. Every second, Radio drifted further and further from life.

"If that's what you want, they're yours, but you help Radio now."

A pleasant smile spread over Allsaint's withered cheeks, never reaching his glass eyes. Why wasn't he doing anything?

He snapped his fingers, the darkness shifted like a living thing. Or several living things. Clammy hands fastened about True. Wrists, ankles, thighs, belly. Cold and pale from life in dark corners. Eliza slipped from their shoulders to their jaw, forcing their head back.

"You're even crazier than me," she whispered, bright with excitement. Out of the corner of their eye they saw Allsaint handing tools to a gnarled shadow dweller. A metal pair of mangled tongs, and a spoon. True dug their nails deeper into the wood. Breathe in, breathe out. Through the mouth, through the nose. Never mind their heart turned their whole body into a laboured pulse. Never mind Eliza pressing bruises into their face.

"Wait!" they gasped, "I want proof it survived. No tricks."

"You'll hear it," Allsaint said.

"It doesn't talk," Eliza said, not a lie. Technically. She met True's stare with a wink.

Humming, Allsaint gave in. "Just the one eye, then," he sounded disappointed, "come now, Eliza, you know I need your steady hands for this."

A warmer, stiffer grip replaced hers. They could feel Cal trembling through their masks, though he had an excellent poker face. Eliza danced to Allsaint's side, and together they turned their backs on True. The pair began to work as the speculum invaded True's right eye.

19
The Eye

It didn't hurt, not the way they were used to, when the spoon slid past their lower lid.

Sickening, the feel of the spoon gliding into the socket. Immense pressure, in their eye, in the sole of their foot, in a thread pulled taut across their body. But not unbearable. Not until their vision split, one screen on Radio and the other on the floor.

Dizzying. Headache splitting. Vertigo seized them and brought with it a volley of retching.

The shadow dwellers held them in place. Eye-thread-foot.

They were almost grateful when the spoon levered and struck the top of their socket with a *thok* that cut off the floor feed. Warmth flooded down their cheek, drenching their hair. And then the pain began in earnest.

Snap—the thread. A hundred thousand fire ants swarmed the clammy, cavernous socket. Biting, burrowing, ripping at the thing lodged there.

Screaming replaced the retching.

Then, a tug.

Then, the cold. Something vital now missing. The gap sucking on dank air.

Then, their other eye went dark, too.

20
The World's Worst Headache

Basement.

Stairs.

Teeth everywhere. Hands everywhere, everywhere.

Ugh, their head hurt.

ɷ

"You should leave soon, Allsaint doesn't—"

"*We* should leave? You look like you haven't slept in a week."

"I haven't."

"This isn't the time for jokes."

"I'm not joking."

"..."

"I've always been sick, Callie, for as long as you've known me. That's what happens to people like me."

"So, what...? You were going to abandon us? Slink off and die alone in your hole? That's a horrible plan! You're a horrible person."

"..."

"..."

"Cal?"

"Yeah?"

"Don't tell Mu."

"Yeah."

"..."

"How long have they been awake?"

"Dunno, hey sunshine."

True blinked slow at the blurry faces of Eliza and Cal. This time they were wedged between sink and tub. Someone else lay in the tub. Drooling, but breathing. Radio had survived.

Eliza was saying something that swam between their ears uselessly. They would have killed for an ibuprofen right then. Prying themself out of the corner, they gripped the rim of the sink and examined the damage. Half their face was stained red. The epicenter, the remnants of their eye, had crusted shut. The lid sagged inward, all loose and floppy now that there was nothing underneath. They poked it, hissed at the searing pain.

Reality burrowed under their flesh. Maggots, bot flies, dredging up panic. Shit, they'd really done that, shit, *shit*.

They smashed the mirror. Had to break something. It wasn't enough. They put another web of cracks in the glass.

Couldn't get their brain to restart.

Someone cleared their throat. True jumped to face the noise. They had to move their whole head to do it. No periphery on that side anymore. Icepick migraine pain lanced their skull from socket to base.

"Do you know where you are?" Cal asked. He leaned on the doorframe, his hands stuffed in his pockets and for a fleeting instant they felt like punching him for making noise. Felt like punching him to make their head stop hurting.

Eliza, rocking back and forth on the toilet lid, cracked a smile that included every one of her sharpened teeth. They jabbed a finger at her and forced words past their stiff jaw. Their own voice vibrated the inside of their head, unbearable.

"If you...talk...I'll kill you."

She batted her eyelashes at them and mimed zipping her lips. Amusement brightened her eyes, but for now at least, she stayed quiet. Crouching beside Radio, True took in its colourless lips and the row of tiny black stitches nestled among its older scars. It shook its head and smushed the heels of its palms into its puffed-up dark-circles eyes.

Okay, time to go. The sooner they got out of the fungus house, the better. They very distinctly recalled Allsaint barging in and dropping them on their bullet wound yesterday. Bracing on the tub edge, they offered Radio their hand. It met them with a limp, uncertain grip.

A minute passed. And then another, and Radio climbed to its feet at the speed of molasses and tipped its head in the faintest of increments all around the room. Its other hand swung lifelessly at its side while True's pulse climbed. That was not the look of someone alive.

"Radio?" they breathed.

At first, nothing. Dull black eyes. Then, a glimmer seemed to return to them. Or maybe that was too hopeful. It could have been a mushroom spore, who the hell knew what terrible feats of decay lingered in that bathroom, planting in its sclera. At the tail end of a very long, very unsteady breath, its brow crumpled, and it grabbed True's chin. Its grip clumsy and cold.

It blinked, this time not a slow one, and at once the mushroom spore glimmer burst into a spotlight. The heat bored holes into them. Into their face. Into their missing eye. It tore apart from them.

Ouch. In the sting of its recoil, they lit it slide out of reach. It hit the wall, bumped into Eliza, and pinballed back into them. Staggering under its weight and their headache, they managed to catch themself on the opposite wall and steady Radio at the same time.

"Let's get out of here," they said. Whatever Radio had to say about the state of their ugly face could be said outside the confines of the cannibal den. No matter how much it scraped at their raw emotions to see it look at them like that.

They adjusted their mask and looped Radio's arm over their shoulders.

"Where are you headed?" Cal asked.

"The first building I can find with a lot of locks and no windows," they answered. "And after that probably to gut that fishery."

And if nothing else they were going to bury a knife in Otsana's heart for what she'd done to Radio.

Cal untucked his hands from his pockets. He'd bitten his nails down to nubs.

"Are you going to punch me again?" True asked with a heavy does of sarcasm.

"No," he said. "Your pack is with Suni."

Damn it.

A shiver went through them, blooming into the sensation of a screwdriver chipping the bone on the inside of their empty socket. They had the world's worst headache and none of this was helping.

"Fine, I'll get that first."

"She's not at the caravan."

Well, why the hell not? Talking hurt too much to waste the words it took to ask that, so instead they said. "Then take me to her."

Cal didn't budge. For a moment, True thought he was going to tell them that he didn't know where she was. But then Eliza squeezed past them and nudged Cal on her way out. "I wanna say hi, too. She was so niiiiice when we were travelling together."

If Cal's eyes rolled any harder they were going to get stuck behind his skull, but he peeled himself off the doorframe and motioned for True to follow.

In the haze of the early morning mist, they walked down the bedewed sidewalk. Radio snuck looks at the empty eye socket, even after True bit a hole in their mask and used a long thread from their sash to pull it up over both new and old scars.

The staring shouldn't have bothered them. They were used to it. Just not from Radio. Did it matter that they were grotesque to it, the way they'd always been to the rest of the world? They glanced at it. A little colour had returned to its cheeks and it was walking on its own. It had handled its impromptu surgery a hell of a lot better than True had.

No, it didn't really matter, it just stung.

There it went again, eyes darting to the covered eye socket. It looked away just as quickly, turning not quite in time to hide a wince.

"Quit that."

It fixed its eyes on the road ahead, only to throw them another side glance, when it thought they weren't looking. They shoved it. It staggered a few steps, mouth open in surprise. It shoved them right back and caught them by the chin while they were off balance. Throwing it off, they stormed away. But it was ready and snagged them by the shoulder before they could escape.

They weren't sure who threw the first punch, but it only took a couple seconds for both of them to be rolling on the sidewalk, grit grinding into hair, fingernails clawing at skin. For an instant, they had the upper hand, pinning Radio to the concrete, then just as quick it heaved off, and landed a kick to their side.

They hit their knees doubled over, agony turning their body into a white-hot pulse. Pain so bright it had snot running down their face cavity.

"Ow, fuckin' asshole!" they groaned.

Taking their face in both clammy hands, it forced them to face it and unhooked the mask. Its lead-weight stare sank into the bloodied socket. Brow knit low over its nose and lips pressed into a thin line, like it was studying the and it didn't like what it was seeing. Funny, because they didn't really like what they were seeing either. True caught it by the wrists and pulled its hands away.

"Don't stare."

Its stern expression softened, much to their disgust. They didn't want its pity any more than they wanted its horror. They'd made their choice, and they'd make it again if time reversed. Radio was just going to have to get over itself.

Shivering, Radio pulled itself free and touched the place Otsana had stabbed it. A question.

"Fair trade," they said, firmly. Wheezed. They walked a thin line between hyperventilating on too-shallow breaths and the molten feeling that clawed their insides when they took a full breath. They ran a thumb over the stitches. All intact.

"You look like a dodo when you sit like that," they muttered when they'd remastered the act of breathing.

As if shaken out of a distant thought, it clicked its teeth together, and reached down to scratch words in the grit.

Run away.

True pushed the back of their hand at it. *No.* Out of the question.

Smacking down onto flat feet, Radio flashed signs at them, a scowl pinching its expression. They cut it off before it worked itself into a frenzy. They hadn't learned enough sing to keep up.

"I'm not leaving until I've finished what I came here for."

It dug its calloused fingers into its scalp.

"I'm burning those fuckers to the ground, Radio."

"Well, now that that's been established."

True flinched at Eliza's sudden appearance on their blind side. She grinned down at them, sharp yellow teeth glinting in the sun. Briefly, True entertained the idea of whacking her with their shovel. Her smile stretched, eyes darkening, like she was reacting to the murder in their thoughts. They caught sight of her fists curling, and reached for a shovel that wasn't there.

Cal's scarred hand clamped down on Eliza's shoulder.

"Your doctor is wandering off," he said into her ear. With a hum, Eliza flicked a scraggle of hair over her shoulder and skipped off the sidewalk, leaving Cal alone to lay his disapproving gaze on True and Radio.

"Do you fistfight everyone?" he asked.

"Yeah," True said, "you're next."

To his credit, Cal didn't take the bait. Though they were dangling it pretty close to his face. And when had Allsaint joined them, anyways?

They straggled to their feet, checked their shirt for blood in case the stitches had burst. Although the shirt they had on was the same one they'd almost died in, so the bullet hole and the dark stain obscured anything else going on under it. It didn't feel like they were bleeding, at least.

Radio was watching them again. They shoved it to the back of their mind. As they pulled their mask up, Radio seized their raised hand to catch their attention.

Pulling a snarl, it tapped their hand once. Then it flashed a thumbs up and tapped their hand twice.

One bad, two good. "Okay," they said, but the meaning didn't sink in until Radio shifted to their right side. Out of sight, but within reach.

Well, it looked like Radio was abandoning the shovel length rule for good. Or at least until it got sick of putting up with them.

Blue sky began to burn through the early morning mist, and Radio reached across the gap between them and tapped twice on their right hand. True bit back the habitual impulse to shoo it away. Instead, they turned their hand over and tapped twice on Radio's palm.

That was going to take some getting used to.

21
The War Room

They slogged through Vancouver's labyrinthine streets of broken concrete and tall grass. There was a little more brick here than on other streets but that hadn't stopped the ivy from eating whole buildings or the tree roots from billowing the roads. Crumbled, disintegrating infrastructure surrounded them. And True left their blood on a fair bit of it because every time they sneezed they speckled whatever was in front of them.

The ornate wooden door of the stiff brick building had propped open with its own handle, which someone had torn off in the process of breaking in. Inside, dust coated a lobby that, dare they say, was timeless.

The polished hardwood floor had no faded stains, the foyer lacked debris, the receptionist's desk bore no graffiti. A law office had nothing a world of starving people wanted. It was almost unsettling how untouched the place was.

The worst of the damage was a bit of broken glass from the tall windows, where raspberries had grown through the panes.

Or it was, until the loudest crash in human history shattered the quiet. True spun, reaching for their shovel, only to see the source of the crash was a red-faced, seething Allsaint. He'd put a computer mouse through an obsolete monitor.

"What is wrong with you," True said at the same time that Eliza swooped in to admonish the doctor with considerably more gentleness.

"Doctor," she chided.

Allsaint threw his shaking hand at the screen. "Damned things not working, and I have to fill out my reports!"

"We don't use computers anymore, Doctor," Eliza said, unusually kind. She snagged an ancient yellow legal pad and a pen from a desk drawer and handed them to the doctor. "We're all physical files here."

Doctor Allsaint frowned at the legal pad and plucked it out of her hands.

Summoned by the racket, Big Valdivia emerged from behind a cherry stained door with a plaque and a name that True didn't care about.

"You scared us half to death," she said, closing the space between them to prop her arm on True's shoulder. Everyone was feeling touch-y today, huh?

They slid out from under her and retreated to the counter. Her gaze traced the new angle of their mask. They let her stew on it, they didn't feel like talking about it now, or ever.

A box of rubber bands collected dust by the broken monitor. How novel. They picked it up. Ugh, they lived in a world where office supplies were novel. It was awfully quiet in there, too. They looked up to three sets of eyes bearing down on them—Allsaint was busy with the legal pad. Creepy.

"I'm here for my pack," they said. Their pack, and maybe these rubber bands.

Valdivia tipped her head at the door she'd popped out from. The windows were shaded, the room beyond it sat dark.

"Great," they said. "Go get it."

"Don't be an ass," Cal started, but Val cut him off with a stiff wave. Just a flick of her fingertips at the end of a squarish robotic hand.

"It's fine, I'll get it." She pivoted, all tense and disjointed, her shoulder lagged half a second behind her hips. They didn't like that the kid was nowhere to be seen, if not because Suni acted untethered and nerve-wracked without her, then because they simply weren't used to seeing mother and daughter out of orbit.

Tilting their head at Cal, they sneered his words back at him. "Don't be an ass."

"You're so right, we balanced a bucket of water on top of that door," Cal said. They almost smirked. Almost. Running their tongue over their crooked teeth to leash the impulse, they let their gaze roam. The lobby seemed bigger than it had at first, they were going to have to get used to turning their head to see all of a place. That was annoying.

"You're missing your third," they said as they peeked under the desk.

Cal settled back on his heels, arms swaying restlessly at his side. Like he was trying to look casual but he was too keyed up to pull it off. "Mu is with the caravan, he didn't need to be here."

Neither did those two shadow dwellers, and yet. "What's his deal?"

"I don't ask about your weird friends."

Fair enough.

A crash and a curse from Valdivia broke the tense, fake calm. Scrunching the remnants of their face into a scowl. True shoved the rubber bands into their pocket and snagged a hefty stapler.

Cal followed on their good side, they knew Radio loomed close on their other side. If all their stuff was on the floor they were throwing this stapler at Big Valdivia's head. Stapler first they poked into the side room.

None of their stuff lay scattered on the rich hardwood. Valdivia lurked at the end of a shellac shiny lake-sized table, nothing in her hands but her own staff. Raised. A second person slinked along the shadows close to the wall.

True hefted the stapler. Their shoulder torqued all wrong as a heavy arm shoved them, the stapler ripped from their grip. Iron whacked their ribcage, True doubled, a bruise sprang to life in the wake of the blow. Door, slammed. Lock, clicked.

They stretched their jaw around a particularly vibrant curse but couldn't manage to spit it out. That was one hell of a bucket of water. The imprint of Valdivia's staff welded itself to their bones as they forced themself upright. Across that impossibly shiny table, they took in a broken noise and swollen lost-lamb eyes.

"You," True snarled.

Jonesy's eyes went as wide as the swelling allowed. In an instant, they were over the table and had Jonesy off the ground. One of the chairs tangled in his legs, crashing him back to the floor. He squawked, flailing to free himself from both True and the chair. That snake, that eel, that little slimy parasite—

Sudden, sharp pain sunflowered over their skull. True threw their elbow back, heard the crunch of it connecting, but the grip on their hair remained adamant. The sting brought tears to their eyes. Eye. Eyes?

"Drop him," Cal said.

"I'm not a dog." True snapped.

"Then stop acting like one."

He wanted to see them act like a dog? They'd show him fucking acting like a dog. From human to cornered animal, they plummeted. They abandoned a clump of hair to Cal's grip and contorted their legs up around his neck. A grunt knocked out of him. He hauled True straight into the path of an unforgiving metal pole.

Splat on the table with a skull full of bells, they got their hands up but not in time to keep the staff from flattening them. Iron crushed their windpipe. Thrashing and wheezing and spitting. They threw their weight one way, bucked back they other. Until stars crowded their vision and sweat turned their skin slippery.

They were not dying in this room, stabbed in the back by people they'd dared to give an ounce of trust, with the whole reason they had dragged their ass out here looming on the horizon.

They croaked, their hips hoisted up above their head only to drop heavy when Cal slipped them. Whack on the edge in time with the whack of the door exploding open. The bar vanished from their throat. Sucking in hungry gulps of dusty air. True scrabbled to their feet. By the time the snow cleared from their eye, the dust had settled on the aftermath of a scuffle. Radio held Valdivia's head to the table, hand pinned high between her shoulder blades and the pinpoint of its knife levelled at her eye. Claw marks radiated from its sneering mouth, and Eliza lingered in the doorway with a trickle of blood oozing from a split over her browbone.

"What happened to keep the shadow dweller busy?" Cal threw his arms to the ceiling.

An enormous crash shuddered the building, dust and probably asbestos rained on their heads. Eliza rocked back on her heels, blinking slow. Behind her, Allsaint heaved with the effort of hurling a computer chair.

"We have rules!" he bellowed, red-faced all the way to the roots of his hair, it seemed even to leak into the whites of his eyes.

"I was busy," Eliza said.

"Unbelievable," Cal said, "I told you to leave him behind, I need this trade. We need food, real food."

True butted in, "you're trading me for a meal?" they worked an appropriate amount of offence into their accusation.

Cal seemed to remember that True was very much alive and in the room. In a move that they were willing to admit was smooth, he kicked Valdivia's discarded staff up to his waiting hand. "I'm only doing what I was hired to do."

And then it was Valdivia's turn to grit her way into the commotion. Her hand was going mauve. "I'm trading you, for my caravan's entry to the Red Faction."

Now that, was unbelievable.

Radio twitched, knife glinted across the table. It burrowed in the wall with a low tuning fork clang. Bony fingers clamped around their ankles. Cal swiped Valdivia's staff and caught True on the back of the knees, leaving them airborne. A wave of stars flushed out their vision and left them blurry on the floor, the staff staked to their temple, a boot grinding into their calf. A waterfall of head-trauma-induced nausea rolled through their body and pulsed at their weak spots.

Too late, they caught Eliza's spidery limbs entering the picture. She bulldozed Radio, her fingers dove into its mouth in a gush of blood and she drove it back into the wall. Drywall dented. Radio shook its head, but she moved as if she hardly noticed, slamming a knee into its groin. Saliva rolled down her arms. And an instant was all the time Valdivia needed to recover. Her arm hung out of its socket, but she snatched a knife from her bet and sucked in a stuttering breath and blinked glassy eyes.

"Valdivia, don't!" They heaved. Couldn't get traction on the hardwood. "I hope your daughter knows you're the one who murdered her," they spit.

Her expression crumpled like a pop can, her knife jerked to a halt. Confusion formed on her chapped lips, cut short when she shied out of the flight path of a keyboard. She ducked in the nick of time, the plastic skimming her curls and shattering on the wall, shards and drywall dust flung into the crowded room.

"What do you mean?" she demanded. They pinched their lips, heat dripping out of their socket. "Get off them."

Jonesy spluttered out a string of noises along the lines of *don't listen to them, just kill them already, blah blah whine whine.* But Cal had released the pressure on their skull long before Jonesy made it to the end of his screeching. Valdivia gripped their shoulder, and judging by the point of the knife angled at their throat, she wasn't holding them for comfort.

"What do you mean I'm killing Kiara?" she asked, enunciating each individual syllable. Nerves locked down every strand of her, except her eyes, which shivered over True's battered face in search of answers.

"The Red Faction kills disabled people," True said. "We watched it happen. At the bridge with—with—" damn it, what had Little Val called that redheaded kid?

"Ali," Cal filled in. His weight lifted from their calf.

"With Ali. You know they killed him. If you join the Faction, your kid will be top of the list to get offed. And Mu, too." Including Mu was a long shot, but they might as well go all in while they were floundering for a way out. They didn't need the whole room to agree with them, they just needed one person to tip the scales.

Jonesy must have sensed the shift in the room's atmosphere. Seizing the lull in the conversation and the face that everyone else had full hands, he gathered his metaphorical petticoats and fled.

The *sk-thunk-WHUMP* of a well-timed wheely chair kicked into his path drummed up to the ceiling panels. Apparently, Eliza had decided other things were more interesting than pinning Radio by its uvula.

"Don't you come near me," Jonesy spit, trying his damnedest to be threatening from his current position as a pathetic mess flumped in the doorway. He choked on his own tongue when Eliza crouched over him. When he cringed at the proximity to her wicked teeth, she hooked him closer by the collar.

"Come to think of it," she said, "the Faction has been poaching our food."

"Don't call people that," Cal interrupted. Eliza rolled her eyes lazily up to him, mouth curved down.

"I meant more than human meat. You know, we don't live on that. In fact, it's a very small part of our diet. Tiny. Miniscule even."

"Okay!"

A chair scraped, the wheeled legs groaned at their first use in close to a decade. The screech sank into the rotted ceiling panels, giving pause to the tumult. Valdivia lifted one finger as if collecting everyone's attention into the torn edge of her nail, and when the level of focus in the room satisfied her, she introduced a new idea to the waters.

"If the caravan and the shadow dwellers work together, we could destroy the Red Faction."

Now there was a plot True could get behind. They caught Radio's stare across the settling dust, tapped their cheek twice. Radio's hand flitted over its stitches, considering. Then it pushed its hand out.

Fine, they'd find some other way to destroy the Faction Not like being ornery and contrarian was anything new. They peeled themself off the floor. Their hip ached and noxious drywall powder colonized the back of their throat. Valdivia aimed her one finger at them. She moved with all the grace of someone whose joints had been spring loaded. If True flicked her with a rubber band, she'd probably end up in the bushes outside.

No, they corrected themself, groaning into a chair of their own, she would probably send them through the wall and into bushes. Plus, she had Cal, and whoever had Cal had Eliza, and any one of them individually had been through two fewer surprise surgeries in the last week and could hold True down with a pinky finger. No thanks, they were better off waiting out the rest of this storm.

The finger of command shifted to the fox woman. Eliza swept her hand towards the doctor.

"The others listen to him, he's the closest thing to a leader we have," she said.

The closest thing the Vancouver shadow dwellers had to a leader stood with his toes to the baseboards while he held his yellow paper pad over his head and scribbled furiously. A frown slid over Valdivia's face. "You mean you're the closest thing you have to a leader."

Bang!

The table rocked back down to four legs, a crack popping into existence on its perfect shiny surface, throwing a puff of dust into the stale air. Dr. Allsaint slammed his notepad down, the pen skittered off into an unused seat.

"Manners!" Foam beaded at the corners of Allsaint's lips.

"Manners," Eliza mouthed.

"He doesn't know what's going on," Big Valdivia said, low and quiet. Electric energy bristled off her, hummed in her words, the way it had once hummed in the dead halogen lights overhead.

Eliza delivered a curtsey so deep she went nose-to-nose with Jonesy. "Interpreter, at your service."

Tapping an uneven staccato with her staff, Valdivia motion for the shadow dwellers to join her at the table. Eliza gave a pleased nod, then hauled back and punted Jonesy's guts.

"You too, tomato boy, get in there."

Slowly the rest of the group gathered around the table. Jonesy took special care to put that table between him and True, so True took care to give him the evil eye at every opportunity.

He'd gotten all sweaty and green around the gills. They picked a rubber band from a pile they were hoarding on their lap and pinged it at him.

Allsaint cleared his throat, tapped his pen. He'd found a new pen, evidently.

"Thank you for your patience, everyone. Patience for patients, patient car, we're here to discuss." He nodded to each of them individually, his doll eyes skirting over their heads. Over Eliza lazing with her elbows propped up on the table and her head lolling between the goalposts of her arms. Over Cal, with his arms folded over his chest while he did a shit job of pretending not to stare at Eliza's jittering hands. Over Valdivia, leaning back in her chair as she drummed her fingers and waited.

True seized the opportunity to prepare another rubber band only to catch Valdivia fixing a mom stare on them, daring them to try something. Bold attitude from someone who'd just tried to murder them. True passed the rubber band to Radio on their blind side.

"Interpreter?" Valdivia settled back into her chair, shoulders tight. When she wasn't looking, they aimed another rubber band at Jonesy's head with malicious intent.

Their Allsaint interpreter had gotten lost in the hypnotic swirl of the dust motes flying through the air. Jaw slack, black bags sagged her lower eyelids down her cheeks and made her look melted and weepy. Cal threw a pen cap at her. It bounced off her forehead and snapped her back into her own head.

A few long slow blinks, a longer, slower smile. For reasons known only to her, she flipped herself onto the table, and each of her vertebrae crackled on the lacquered surface. True felt it in their teeth. Yuck. She came to a crouch in front of Radio.

"Shadow dwellers don't deal with outsiders."

It didn't matter who said what next, Radio's fingers were digging into True, and that was their signal to leave. Tilting back in the chair, they kicked Eliza's shin. She staggered, then pounced, teeth bared.

Whoops. One foot in the air, True kicked away from the table, rubber band hoard scattering, only for Radio to snatch Eliza out of the air and slam her to the floor. Uttering an undignified yelp, she gripped its hair and heaved it down with her. That was True's cue. Stomping on her wrist, they bent, pried her fingers loose. Pinning her other arm with her knee left them free to grab her by the chin—out of reach of her fangs.

"Hot," she said, grinning. Chest heaving, blood on her teeth.

"Ugh."

"Eliza!" With one word, Cal snapped her whole focus to him. "What does that mean?"

Nobody moved, paralyzed by the weight of the unspoken answer. They all knew what it was. Or at least, True knew. They could see Radio out of the corner of their eye, rubbing the crooked line of its mouth with a bloodless white knuckle.

Allsaint spread his fingers wide. "We are cannibals, after all." It was, unfortunately, the most lucid thing he'd said all day. Chaos erupted.

Or tried to. The table rocked under Valdivia's fists, quelling the fresh sparks of dissent. She let the quiet hold for a beat. Tension strung her tighter than an overwound analog clock, and by the way she tracked an invisible line from Jonesy to True, and back again, True could tell what sort of calculations were going on inside her head.

They were doing their own math, too, Over the thunder of their own strained heart in their ears. Tapping to fingers like a gun to Eliza's forehead they said, "Ill."

Allsaint. "Ill."

Radio. "Off limits."

Cal.

"Off limits." Eliza gave an exaggerated frown. True wasn't about to argue with that.

"Count me out, too," Jonesy huffed, "I'm not getting snacked on."

"Shut up, Jonesy," True said.

Maybe it was the lightheadedness catching up to them, the way the room had been swimming lazily in and out of focus for the past eight or ten minutes. Maybe it was just that they'd forgotten their field of vision was half gone. But they didn't notice until too late that his voice hadn't come from where it was supposed to be.

They whipped towards his voice, towards Radio, pulling fire into their lungs. It clutched its knife, but moved like it was pushing through honey. Sticky with panic. And before Radio could shake the panic attack, before True could close the gap,

Jonesy drove its skull into the wood. The hollow crack of the abused tabletop echoed in True's head, and Radio's mouth fell open to suck in a ragged gasp.

"You listen," Jonesy jabbed his words not at True, but at Valdivia. Grabbing a fistful of Radio's hair, he whipped its head to the side, exposing the scarred flesh of its neck to his knife. Behind the flowered bruises, his eyes couldn't rest. Not jittering, the way shadow dwellers did, but shifting always away. "I've been in the Red Faction, I'll tell you whatever you want to know if you give me a place in your caravan. But I'm walking out of here with all my body parts regardless."

Valdivia rocked on the balls of her feet. She'd done nothing to stop him from getting to Radio, and now her gaze slid back to True.

"Final offer, you have ten seconds—"

"Shut up, Jonesy," True and Valdivia spoke at the same time. Her knuckles popped around her staff.

"Guess that just leaves you," she said.

"Guess it does."

She landed back on her heels, but True held up their hands to put a stop to the motion in the room before it could stir up too far. "For a trade."

The cook sputtered a few broken syllables of indignation, but True was already giving their own terms.

"You treat Radio like a civilian," they said. "And I want in on taking down the Faction."

A beat. Valdivia nodded. That was settled, then. Radio was shaking its head, but the room had already broken into motion, and Eliza snapped in True's face to draw their attention. She fanned her nails out in front of True, as if displaying them. She'd filed those into sharp points, too, they noticed.

"Aw, True," she sighed, and plunged her pointed nails through their stitches. "You're so much fun."

With a soft grunt, True slumped. Freezer burn spread from the impact point. It hit their head, turning the room hazy in half-second pulses. Pulse, the eerie sensation of falling backwards tripped through them. Pulse, Radio had its arms around them, pulling them off Eliza. Her hand shiny and red up to her second knuckles.

Well, that was settled then.

Digging in the inner pocket of their coat, they found the prescription bottle from before everything had gone downhill. That felt like years ago now. They shoved the azithro into Radio's nearest pocket.

"Nothing I need to live," they warned.

"Promise," Eliza said, patting the table.

True bit a ragged line into the soft flesh of their cheek as hands pinned them to the smooth, cold table. Sweat soaked through to True's skin, rewetting the salt cooling there. Gross, they grimaced.

"Get over here, vet lady, you're his hands." Eliza pointed Valdivia to Allsaint's side.

"Aren't you his nurse?" Valdivia said. In answer, Eliza held up her hands to show off an uncontrollable tremor. New symptom. True watched the way Cal lingered on it, something sad and hopeless creased the space between his brows on his otherwise neutral face. They wondered if they ever looked at Radio like that. Or was it Radio who looked at them, while they traded away pieces of themself over and over.

The midday sun turned the drywall dust in the air into a shimmering powder. Pretty, if a little toxic. A ray settled over Dr. Allsaint's unnerving pale eyes as he lumbered toward them. Quiet now, almost serene. He hadn't managed to kill them the first two times, True reminded themself as the doctor peeled their bloodstained shit from their lurching skin, their belly fluttered with each too-short breath. A river of warm blood slithered down their side to pool on the table.

Fuck, this was going to hurt.

Radio took their hand on their blind side and squeezed once.

22
The Hollow

Blood coagulated on the shiny table lip. A tendril stretched to the floor, drawing itself longer and thinner and thinner and longer. A bulb at its end swirled and weighed it lower yet. Until the spider-silk-thin tendril snapped and landed with a plip on True's boot.

Their body burned.

Vomit—Cal's—cooled in the corner. Dark crimson slabs lay on the torn covers of hardback books, oozing red from spongy meat.

True had eaten kidney once or twice. Cow kidney. Theirs looked different. Smoother, a darker shade of red.

Big Valdivia dropped her face into her hands.

"Now," Dr. Allsaint tutted, but trailed off, the light in his eerie pale eyes glazing over. True figured their gaze was pretty glazed, too. Hollow on the inside. Hollowed out from the inside.

Valdivia began to tremble, and Cal, the only normal one in the room, rubbed her hunched back and murmured something that made her shake her head.

"She can never know about this." Her voice carried the same sound as the wind shuddering through fragile autumn leaves.

True watched her, Cal watched her. Eliza watched her, pouting. At last, Valdivia straightened and cleared her throat.

Eliza's pout transformed into a soulless grin. "Bon appétit to a new alliance," she proclaimed, and popped her hunk of kidney into her mouth.

True moved slow. Didn't mean to, it was just hard to move. Or think. Kidney, wet, smooth. Like sponge, like solidified mashed potatoes. Brought it to their lips, stomach churned. Static in the head. This was wrong wrong wrong wrong wrong—

It tasted of iron and bitterness, and slid down the back of their gullet wrong.

Dark red smudged the corner of Radio's mouth. That was the first time they'd ever seen it eat. Really eat, not a licorice snack. It looked as gone as True felt. Rubbed at the smudge robotically. Its eyes lit on True, focused. With twitching lips, it lifted both hands, and mimed eating a corncob. Wrong, wrong reaction.

True snorted. That asshole. Laughter creeped out of them. High-pitched, breathless, vocal cords fried from screaming. Radio's shoulders started to shake. It hurt to laugh, scorched them from stomach to throat. They choked, hacked out a glob of mucus and blood. Threw their head back, tears ran down their cheeks. Dissolved into hysterics.

Blood warmed their side. And they laughed. And the burned raged in the hollow wrong pit in their body. And they laughed until all that was left was dark and void.

23
The Void
The Void
The Void

Lying on their back in a cold grey room, staring up at the silhouette of a gargoyle on the windowsill, they came back into their body. They exhaled. Their breath tasted like dust and their mask was missing.

Okay, what else?

Not dead, check.

In a strange place, check.

They sat up—*ow*.

Sore everywhere, check. A ragged line on their stomach glowed and angry pink. A phantom shifted in their empty eye socket, scratching the inside of the lid. They picked at a strand of hair that had coiled inside and popped the wad out. Pleasant, they grimaced, holding up the slimy ball. Eight tiny eyes glittered back at them. With a curse, they flung the spider. It hit the wall with a *thok* and skittered into the shadows. Shuddering, they scrubbed their empty socket with their sleeve.

"I can't believe you let a spider live in my eye," they grumbled. The gargoyle, Radio, unfolded its legs. "A spider. Alive. Living in my eye."

Radio threw its arms around them, pressed its face into the crook of their neck. Their pulse thrummed on its cheek. That was a lot of touching for that soon after waking up.

They folded it into themself.

"Okay, alright, I'm not dead, big deal." They gave Radio one last squeeze before pulling away.

A spot of wavering yellow backlit the water stained sheet hung over the entryway. It leaked over the debris-littered floor, swelling into a globe when Big Valdivia ducked into the room. A stubby tallow candle cast her face in gloomy relief. She stalled in the doorway when she saw them, rocking back on her heels with a sharp breath.

Hm, well, look at that. Hate felt cold when it burned that bright.

Hand curling tight on the sheet, Big Valdivia landed on flat feet and entered. The candle flame wobbled hard as she set it next to an empty prescription bottle on a warped table that had been shoved into the corner.

"I'm not sorry for what I did," she said. In the wavering light she looked scarecrowish, thinner than she had in the legal office. Nothing like the woman who had nearly caved their head in, unfortunately. That woman had been ready to tear apart the Red Faction.

"Good for you." They hoped the rasp in their voice carried the indulgent volume of sarcasm they intended. Valdivia might need that conversation, but they didn't, unless it came imbued with the magical ability to un-cannibalize their kidney.

Testing their legs, they pried themself off the disintegrating spring mattress. A rush of static blurred their vision and threatened to wash their limbs down the drain. Radio pressed a supportive hand to their back. They waved it off. They could walk, they just needed time. With a slow exhale, the lightheadedness passed.

They were mostly intact. Horrifically sore, like they'd been hit by a train once or twice. Standing up, walking, moving in general pulled at the tender patch in their side and sent their brain into a dizzy spiral.

A hollow place hid under the topography of their belly. Nothing underneath. Nothing there. Just nothing.

But they could walk. They rested their weight on the table, skimming its contents. A dozen terrible bundles of plastic and metal lay in four neat groups long the back of the table. Scraps and rusted tools and makeshift tinfoil dishes holding the remnants of stuff True couldn't even begin to guess at had been pushed to the sides to make room for hand sketched blueprints and pages of bullet-pointed instructions on the backs of browning receipts. They recognized the handwriting.

Flammable materials, said Radio from the crumbling paper.

"We're burning them," True approved.

"We're blowing them up," Valdivia said.

So that's what the bundles were. Very poetic, considering. They lifted one, listening to the rattle. Light caught an R scratched into one flattened side. The other side had a stick figure family aggressively crossed out.

"A little different from firefighting," they said, casting Radio a wry look. It gave a half-hearted ta-da. "Are these okay to have around fire?" they asked, eyeing the stubby candle. Suddenly it didn't seem like such a good idea to be standing so close to the table. Valdivia snagged the candle out from Radio's reaching fingers.

"I've got it," she said, too quick. Whispers of the return of her springlock joints coiled her grip tighter about the candle.

Cracking a grin, True pinched the wick out. "You have a lot of nerve treating Radio like that after our trade. After what you did to me?"

'Mom!"

True snapped their mouth shut on their next sentence. Teeth sank into tongue, a rush of blood coated the inside of their cheeks. Big Valdivia's wide eyes shone out of the murk, glued to True. Her daughter teetered off the last step to Big Valdivia's side, a dirty plastic bagful of crinkly bottles swinging off her arm. Mu trailed after her, Cal at his side.

"We got so many bottles," Little Valdivia said, letting her mother wrap a protective arm around her.

"Good job, honey," Big Valdivia said, a tremor in her voice. She cleared her throat to cover it and dug something out of her pocket and held it out to True. "I hope it's a start."

True rolled the translucent orange plastic in their palm. "An empty bottle. Thanks."

"It had antibiotics in it," Big Valdivia said. "Radio needed some."

They rolled the plastic bottle over again, an illegible worn label stared up at them. The decided to say nothing. Let her squirm for a day, a fee for emotional labour, since they sure weren't going to be sleeping easy any time soon. The nightmares from this were going to be a bitch.

Big Valdivia smoothed her daughter's hair away from her face, prying her faze off True.

"Moooom," Kiari fidgeted under the touch. Suni batted her softly.

"It's in your face," she said.

"I like it like that." Little Val protested.

"You like to make your mom tired." Big Val worried her lip, wincing when her skin cracked. She studied her daughter's face like this was the last time she would ever get to see it, which did not fil True with confidence in this bomb plot. "Show me what you and Mu got."

Summoned by the sound of his name, Mu shrugged a duffel from his shoulders. The contents of the bag crinkled as he set it down. Radio joined him at the table to peer at the loot. It plucked a clear plastic bottle from the pack and tossed it over its shoulder. The bottle thumped True's shoulder. Fumbling, they caught it. Clear liquid sloshed inside the grimy old water bottle, obviously not water. The stench of alcohol singed True's nose hairs through the seal. Ugh, that was strong. They held it away from their face before the burn could make their eyes water.

"I don't think that's edible," they said, tossing the bottle of moonshine.

"It's fire fuel," Cal said from out in the hall. "Congrats, you're on the bomb squad."

"Sounds tiring."

"Go back to sleep, then."

True tugged their mask up to cover a snort. That wasn't even funny. They did want to go back to bed, thinking about climbing those stairs made them pre-emptively exhausted.

"Me and who?" they asked.

"Radio and Eliza." He rocked back on his heels, biting his tongue. Okay, True and Eliza. That was a group they could tolerate. They didn't trust Eliza farther than they could spit, but she'd do her job.

"And?"

Three people, four sets of bombs. Cal smacked flat onto his feet, the sound echoed in the absence of an answer. Only two people unaccounted for, and Cal sure as hell wouldn't be stalling on Mu's name.

"Jonesy is the only one who's been inside the fishery," Big Valdivia started.

Who cared how he'd gotten inside in the first place, right? True slammed the moonshine on the table, shoving past Mu. A Market buzzed above them, the only way out was up, through the crowd.

Cal cut from their left, which gave them time to brace, snarl. Radio intercepted him none too gently. His knuckles smacked off the cinderblock wall, shoe scraping on the lip of the step. With a sharp breath, he steadied himself on the nearest option—Radio.

True didn't even think his fingers closed all the way before he hit the bottom of the stairs. He rolled to a crunchy halt as Radio retreated up a step, a quiver in its flaring nostrils.

"Hey!" Mu boomed. His moony face crumpled with equal parts distress and anger as he swung his long, floppish body up the stairs. One step too close and he crunched, too. Little Val's shriek harmonized with Mu's yelp when he hit the wall head on. Blood burst from his nose, his arm popped, wrenched up between his shoulder blades. The whites of Radio's eyes flashed. Its chest heaved up, down, on sharp exclamation point breaths.

Above, the hubbub of the Market swelled, drawn by the commotion.

"Control your—"

"Control my *what*," True cut Big Valdivia off, daring her to say what she meant. The ache in their side flared in time with their racing pulse. "You really want to pretend you're better than us? We made a trade."

"True—" panic painted her voice neon bright. She pushed her daughter behind her as if she could shield Little Val from the truth. Her stare dropped to True's hollowed-out side. Yeah, that's right. One bad trade. When she lifted her eyes, the panic had gone cold. A small part of them cowered from her. They understood the Suni that had come out to play in that law office conference room, but they hated her for it.

"Radio," they said, measured and quiet.

Radio Silent unstuck itself from Mu's whimpering bulk. The thin thin line of its lips on the verge of pressure fusing. Grinding a worm of fear between their molars, True jerked their head at the exit. They didn't know where they were going but it had to be away from here. Radio fell into step beside them. Pinching their sleeve to catch their attention, it tapped the tips of its shaking fingers to its chin and drew them down to its waiting palm.

"I'm fine," they grumbled, laying a steadying hand on its cold back. Their cheeks stung. Were—why were they smiling? Not smiling, they tested the corner of their mouth with their tongue. Baring their teeth.

At the top of the stairs, the crowd parted, repelled by their anger. And yet it was suffocating. The nearness of all those bodies pushed on their skin, and it felt like dirt piled onto their grave.

"I never agreed to do things your way," Valdivia's call froze them in place. She stood at the foot of the stairs, from that distance they almost couldn't make out her overwound joints or the anger sharpening the planes of her face. "Only to let you join us. There's no time to change plans now."

Join them. *Join* them. True sneered, balling the hem of their tattered shit in their hand. They bared their tender, deep pink scar. Still held shut by dental floss stitches. Still weeping and mottled.

"I'll have to trade you my other kidney to get a vote, eh?"

Shock rippled through the crowd, pushing it apart at the seams. Valdivia, for her part, swayed. A little limp. A little unbalanced. Her anger plastered on her face like a theater mask. It looked like her springlocks had finally snapped.

Shoving their hands into their pockets, True turned to escape out the gaps of the split-apart crowd before the aftermath caved in on Valdivia and trapped them down there with her.

One night. Fine.

They would deal with these people for one more night. Unlike Big Valdivia, they honoured their trades. And anyways, those bombs were all they had to rip the Red Faction to shreds. To make it so the Faction would never come after Radio—or True—again.

24
The Beginning of the End

Ugly purple clouds billowed over the ocean, turning the waves dark and sharp. Light crackled between the crevices. Wind drew the storm closer, carrying on it the prickle of ozone and sea salt.

The simmering orange bubble of the sun sank below the seething ocean. Foam coated the overgrown banks and clung to the barnacles clumped on the dilapidated bridge. True was trying not to focus on the way the bridge swayed. They crouched in the growth, waiting. Their pack weighed on their shoulders, comfortable and grounding, although their possessions had all been removed to make room for Radio's explosives. They held their shovel across their lap, a water bottle of moonshine hung from their belt, and a shard of glass hid under their sleeve, bound to their arm by a stretch of old cloth.

Radio Silent crouched on their blind side. They kept Jonesy well within their sighted side, and Eliza perched somewhere behind them in a tree, chewing on something that True felt was better not to ask about.

The plan was simple.

Thin the Red Faction's numbers by luring them out to a false After Market.

Launch a shadow dweller attack at the bridge.

Swim across to the island and plant the bombs.

Somewhere north of the bridge, Cal walked the spider-silk thin line of an alliance that would be dead by the end of the night, regardless of which side won. He and half the civilians were biting their blades, sharing war space with Allsaint and his coven of dwellers until the time came to spring the trap.

Across the city, at the false After Market, waited Big Valdivia and the rest of the civilians.

True rubbed the trench in their side. The jab of pain focused them. It was hot to the touch and cramped something fierce. Unsurprising. They'd caught infections from cleaner, smaller injuries. It wasn't going to kill them in the next few minutes, so they shoved it way back under a pile of other things they were ignoring. Like that bridge. And the deep ache in their head that felt like a railway tie being pounded through their eyeless socket.

"There they go," Eliza whispered. Sure enough, strutting along the bridge was a mini horde of factioneers. They walked in silence, the scuff of their patched clothes and clomp of their boots were the only sounds they made. No *sk-flps*, True noted with a fair share of bitterness. They squished as far down into the underbrush as they could get. Held their breath as the factioneers marched past, eye sharp.

There, bringing up the rear, Otsana's obnoxious white-streaked hair. Good, she would come home to smoldering ruins, the way they had, if she came back at all.

A twig snapped.

True's glare whipped toward the sound. Enemy? Wild animal? Stranger? Jonesy. True tried to kill him with their thoughts. Jonesy made a show of cringing and easing off the stick crushed under his knee. The psychic murder attempts redouble.

Turning a watchful eye on the factioneers, they tightened their grip on their shovel. The group marched on, miraculously unaware of the ambushers a mere few feet from them. All except one. Otsana had slowed, dropping off the tail-end of the pack. She skimmed the clumps of brush where True hid. True's hand drifted to a backpack strap, preparing to shed the extra weight.

After a long, sweat-soaked pause, Otsana turned her back and ran to catch up to her group. A minute ticked by, five minutes. True dared not move. The anticipation of the horde turning back kept their heart in their throat. But the factioneers blurred into silhouettes and finally disappeared.

When the factioneers showed no signs of re-appearing. True snake their hand out to catch Jonesy.

"What the fuck is wrong with you?" they hissed.

"It was an accident!"

"Well next time, why don't you *accidentally* set off the bombs. It will kill us faster."

Jonesy twisted out of their grip and stumbled out of reach.

"Come on, boy and others." Eliza thumped down to Earth, cat-like. She stuck her hands out and made like she was patting their heads. True air-ducked the air-pat and scowled at her back as she skulked to the water and sank in without so much as a shudder. Hair fanned out like an oil spill on the soft waves and her package of bombs hoisted precariously over her head, she struck out for the other shore. Radio slithered in after her.

Gruff and grumbling, True dug the first of their own supplies from their pack and crouched by the base of the bridge. On the opposite shore, Eliza chasséd toward her side of the bridge, drawing a wicked-looking knife from her waistband. Where had she gotten that? It was a nice knife. She gave it a theatrical twirl before pouncing on the factioneer that had come out to check on the noise.

"Are you sure you can see well enough to set that up?" Jonesy whispered.

"If you talk to me again, I will throw you in the water." True said. They heard his teeth click shut. He did have an operational brain cell after all. Would have been nice if he'd put it to use earlier. Say, three weeks earlier.

Jonesy's clammy hand squeezed their shoulder, "That After Market was my home, you know," he said in a whisper laden with grief.

The skin beneath the protective layer of their jacket crawled where he clutched them. Twilight hid the revile creeping over their face. There was something thick and rotten in the way his eyes darted to the shadows, in the way he leaned into True, that made their hackles prickle.

"We're not that different, True. I haven't made great choices to get here, but you know what its like, you were out there too. You went a little mad, too. I just needed a way out."

The tip of the glass shard threatened to break skin. They clenched a fist, unclenched the fist. They could see it now, that missing piece of the puzzle that had evaded them for so long. That Jonesy didn't just need to survive, he needed to survive *with* someone.

They stood, knocking Jonesy's hand from their shoulder. So close, too close.

"Maybe you're right," they whispered low, low, low. Maybe they were mad, maybe they need someone to survive with. And who could blame them if all that was true?

They jerked their chin at the island and skirted past Jonesy to clomp as quietly as they could down the soggen bank. Frigid water sucked the breath from their throat. Down they sank, letting the cold snap over them in tight bands. The salt stung in their wounds. Muck suctioned their heavy shoes deeper into the ocean bed. If they stayed there, would the become a milky eyed, salt crystal fixture of the decaying landscape? They pushed for the island shore.

Splashing followed them, the cook handled the chill with less grace than the cannibals that had gone before. At least he muffled his swearing. True poured their focus into keeping their pack above water. A hundred pounds of steel-toed caps and waterlogged clothes and weary bones dragged them to the depths with every kick. Saltwater kicked up their nose, a hot acid shot to the brain, instinct jerking their head back with a snort.

And then they hit the shore, clawed their way on. It was steep here, the silt falling away under their weight. They had to heave their pack up into the bushes to use both their arms and haul themself onto land. They stopped for a minute to peel down their mask and wrestle with their sleeve. It had caught on the shard. Slimy foam and decaying wet grass dried on their coat.

Behind them, splashing. They pulled the mask into place, turned, and motioned for Jonesy to hoist his pack to them. They thought they could make out his lips forming the words "thank you". How easy would it be to leave him there to struggle, alone. But they needed those bombs in his pack, wobbling just out of reach.

"Jonesy," they said. He goggled their way, startled by the sound of his own name. Snagging the strap of Jonesy's pack, they stuck their shard of glass between his ribs. A quick snap, a grunt. They pushed him beneath the surface to smother the sound, bubbles trilled in its place. Moonlight glittered off the fragile, pearlesque domes before they burst and let Jonesy's last breath escape. The dark water swallowed his blood.

They should have fed him to the cracked prairie asphalt. Oh well, hindsight and all that. They hooked his pack and theirs and turned to hike up the shore. Behind them the gravel crunch of battle splattered the night air.

The fishery bulged over them, the reek of long-gone eviscerated fish thickened the heavy air and made the man-made island swampish with rot. Waiting at the top of the rise, Radio stood in the shadow of the bloodred medic symbol, eyes slanted down at True. They faced each other in the quiet while the oncoming storm heaved the ocean and sky into chaos.

Radio unfurled one finger, pressed it to its lips, and gestured for them to join it.

According to Jonesy, rest his soul, the main factory was the only building in use, except for a small shed on the far end of the island that stored the Faction's main claim to fame: medicine. They weren't blowing that up.

True's original drop spots were inside the factory. Ground floor, and down in the basement where the generators ran. And Jonesy's had been on the second floor, in a gutted area he'd referred to as the bunks.

Now, staring up at the skeletal, hole-riddled outer walls of the floors high about their head, True felt a faint twinge of regret. But they were past getting to indulge in that feeling.

Creaking metal and the clink of chains smacking together filled the air, the factory swayed above them, a teetering tower. Sheets of rust flaked off the deteriorating walls and lamps had been hung sparingly along the main path, illuminating little except proof that the stretches of dark between them led in a straight line. Every once in a while another light glimmered deep to the left or the right as True and Radio passed.

Voices trickled from one of them. True paused to confirm that the voices weren't moving closer. Eliza had done her job well, taking out the watches silently, quickly. The factioneers wouldn't know about the enemies slinking through their base until it was too late. As long as no one fucked up.

One kerosene lamp later, they reached a split where the dark eased to a dingy green and the ceiling fell away. True tipped their head back, a set of stairs on their right stretched all the way to the third floor, and a ceiling that had been tarped over. Raindrops struck the beginning of a drumbeat on the tarp, a few stray drops of water clung to the metal grate steps.

A drop fell, glittering, straight onto their forehead. Cold on their hot skin. They wiped it off and turned to trudge down the corridor opposite the stairs. Generators first. Anything to put off leaving the stable ground.

Cement steps formed a gullet into the unlit basement. A deep purr-hum rose from the depths, and a strange, out-of-sync burble. For all the world, True could only picture a headless giant choking in slow motion, his last wet coughs distorted down to those low burbles. They descended, a trapped cloud of the dead fish reek enveloped them in its gases. Mildew, a hint of diesel, and the putrid meat stench of an infection left to fester. Oily stink beaded on their tongue, drawing a cough from them. Behind, Radio stopped to gag.

"My time to shine," they mumbled, mostly to distract themself from the squelch. Sparking their lighter seemed like a bad idea, given the gas smell. They fished it out of their coat pocket and thumbed the spinner. Once, nothing. That dip in the ocean had soaked it. Right. They gave it a shake and flicked it again. Weak orange light sprang forth to glimmer off the damp patches on the concrete basement surfaces and the round glass belly of a lamp.

Orange swelled to a dilute yellow bubble that slicked over a forest of swaying rusted chains and clear tubing. Dark puddles lay beneath the tubes, and off to True's left, a pipe jutting from the floor belched thick, black ooze. That same black ooze crushed a bloodless hand to the heavy grates of the drainage trench they stood on and squeezed onto the floor in soft chunks. They stepped over it and followed the hum to the generators.

Generators. Bombs. Done. They zipped their bag to leave and turned to see Radio broaching the edge of their bubble with one arm tight to its face. It waved its free hand at the basement stairs. A second bubble of light swelled from the exit, growing larger each passing second. Damn it. Swapping their own lamp for their shovel, they darted back through the ooze with Radio. The generator hum covered their splashing steps and the thud of their shoulder hitting the cinderblock wall as they flattened themself to it.

"Shut up, we have to check the gens anyways. I don't want to be stuck here with no refrigeration when the solar panels fly off."

"Why? It already stinks... was Dave down here earlier?"

"What? No."

"But the light—"

Shit, they'd left the lamp lit.

Planting their foot, True swung. Metal met metal with a jostling clang that drove them back. Radio darted into the opening to snag factioneer number one and yank her down into the muck. Recovering, True side-stepped into the light, straight into a gut punch. Vomit splashed the back of their throat. They jammed the shovel handle up into factioneer number two's chin. A hand rose from behind, grabbed them, they let the full weight of their body slam into factioneer number one. Heard a crunch. Debated through a headful of stars whether it was their shoulder or the factioneer's.

They took a hit. Another hit. Threw their head back, cracking their skull into factioneer number one's face. Static burst across their eye and they kicked out, made contact. Kicked again. By the third kick the static had cleared and both factioneers were on the ground, unmoving.

Leaning over, they spit a mouthful of sour bile. Radio wiped a smear of blood from its nose and stomped out the lamp. Two bombs down, two to go.

25
The Second Floor

At least the stairs had handrails. And there were only five million steps. Wind and rain made the ceiling tarp dance and strain against its restraints. The second-floor door, a thing of steel and long-since fogged wire mesh windows, had been wedged open. They stepped into the relative safety of the hall. The floor transformed from groaning metal grates to solid concrete layered with peeling click-lock vinyl. Once again, the echo of voices gave True pause. High-pitched laughter. Children's laughter.

Grouching, they shoved the bomb back into their pack and trudged deeper into the second floor. The click-lock sagged under their weight as if the concrete below it had dissolved, and the lighting was sparser than it had been on the ground floor. They passed more unlit lamps.

The first fork in the road gave away the children's position. Halfway down the westward hall, was the brightest room in the entire place. Shadows flitted across the lit square cast from the door and hushed voices danced from the opening. They motioned for Radio to check the opposite hall and tread on, trying not to make any extra noise.

At the lip of the door, they clipped their shovel in place and pulled down their mask. Lunging into the room, they grabbed the closest child, the biggest, no more than twelve or thirteen. By the time the laughter cut off, they had the child pinned to the wall by the throat. She scratched at their arm, face turning a startling shade of purple. Whoops. They let up the pressure until they heard her gasp.

"How many other children are here?" they demanded, turning their vicious monster stare on the younger children cowering behind a bunkbed.

"It's just us," the pinned child cried, "just us three. You're hurting me." Fat tears rolled down her cheeks, her trembling hands struggled to keep a grip on True's arm. They dug their dirty fingernails into the calloused flesh of their palm.

"You have five minutes to pack your things and leave."

"B-but—"

"Nobody is coming to help you. Five minutes." They dropped the child. She stumbled out of arm's reach, folded inwards. The other children, two in total, rushed forward to clump around her.

She reached for something in her pocket and whirled on True, knife blade leading the way. True batted it out of her hand. She cried out, clutching her arm to her chest. The glare she gave them from under tear-soaked eyelashes was filled with hate. But True was bigger and meaner, and a hell of a lot scarier than anything she'd ever met.

They grabbed one of the smaller children clinging to her, ignoring the cries.

"You know where food and water are?"

The kid nodded so fast their head nearly bobbled off.

"Take your bag and go get as much as you can. If you don't come back your friends will die." They released the kid and watched them scramble out of the room, a backpack crushed to their body like a shield. True counted out five minutes, ticking off the numbers silently on their fingers. It helped keep the pit in their stomach at bay. They hadn't expected there to be children here.

Although, in hindsight, that had been a stupid assumption. Of course the Red Faction had children, and it was too late to back off now. The bombs were almost all set. All they could do was force these kids out and terrify their fragile kid brains too much to even think of coming back.

At minute four the two kids scurrying around the room had finished cramming all their possessions into packs. True beckoned them over, shrugging their own pack off. They opened the pack to show the children the explosives.

"These are bombs," they said, "there are ore everywhere in this building. I'm going to blow these up and everyone in here will die, understand?"

The children nodded, slow, wide-eyed.

"If you don't tell me and there are other kids here, they will die," True warned.

"No one else is here!" the oldest answered, sounding small and full of anger and hurt.

True snapped the pack shut as the last kid returned with their backpack stuffed full. Radio appeared, wraithlike, in the doorway. True pointed to it.

"That's Radio, it's a shadow dweller." They gave their statement a second to take root, watching terror spawn anew on the children's faces. "Radio is going to take you over the bridge and you better not come back. And if you even think about giving Radio trouble, it will eat your fingers."

Ignoring the scowl Radio shot them over the heads of the kids, they marched the whole herd to the stairs. Sent them clambering down. Watched until the kids slipped out the same door True had snuck in. One, two, three, and Radio. That was all they could do.

Turning their back, they knelt just inside the door to lay the third bomb.

Stepping back onto the nerve-wracking metal death trap, they steeled themself for the climb. A crack of thunder rattled the fishery. Grinding their teeth, they tightened their vise grip on the railing. The tarp snapped and billowed, raindrops slapped the cement.

At the third landing, the tarp tore free and at once the storm was inside. Torrential rain and howling wind body-slammed True at the same time. The stairs shuddered, throwing them against the rail. Cursing, they found the lip of the next step with their knees and squeezed their eyes shut.

As if this night needed to be any more difficult.

Okay, they exhaled out their nose, prying a hand off the rail to pull up their mask. All they had to do was make it up one more flight, cross a catwalk, and plant the last bomb. In a downpour. With the very steps they walked on rattled. And then make it all the way back down. Great. No problem.

Another slow exhale, and they set their hand farther up the handrail. Put the other hand over that one. First hand over the second one. On and up straight to the top. Eyes squeezed shut. Traitorous limbs threatening to give out and send them tipping over the slick railing.

Splat, True pancake.

Would the bombs go off when they hit the ground?

They had to pry their eye open to find the next leg of the journey; the catwalk. It spanned a cavernous gap, open air on all four sides. The bare roof and a long stretch of what had once been windows but was now a skeleton offered no protection from the gale. Warm light flickered in the window of the closed third-floor door, inviting them in from the storm.

They stepped onto the catwalk. Sheets of rain sliced at them, wind eddied furiously through the metal fishery bones. *Look down*, it screeched, *face your fate*. The siren call of the ocean rose to a scream. True silently added oceans and hurricanes to the list of things they never wanted to see again.

Halfway across. The land beyond the empty windows lay under a blanket of shadow until, at once, it didn't. True faltered, phobia squashed in the wake of a brilliant gout of orange that turned the caravan warehouse into a pocket of midday sun. The After Market's blaze lit the night, smoke as thick and dark as the thunderheads billowed from the flames.

Something had gone wrong.

26
The Fear of Heights Justified

Howling wind tore the door from the rain-slick hand. The handle punched a hole in the wall and stuck, the homey lamp glow spluttered. They sloshed into the stretch of hall, too grateful for solid ground and relief from the storm to notice the woman in the office chair at the end of the hall.

"Nice of you to join us," the woman spoke, looping a short length of soft, red tubing around her finger. Pink stained the white streak in her hair, a manic flush painted her pale cheeks.

"Otsana," they said, breathless from the climb, tracking the end of the tube burrowed in her arm to a mass dangling from the rafters. A bright red medic patch glared down at them.

"You know he made it eight weeks without any of us noticed he was deaf? Imagine if he'd been up here on his own, you could have snuck right past him." Otsana said, flickering a smile that held not a hint of amusement. She uprooted the needle from her arm and let it drop to drool a slow puddle on the vinyl.

"I have to ask." They gestured to the tubing. Their shovel dangled at their elbow, could they unclip it faster than she could close the gap? Darkness settled over Otsana, cleaving lines over her expression. She leaned closer, different now from the woman who'd stood over them in the empty house. Full of cracks, bits of her leaking out.

"Hrōkr told me all the way here to bash your brains in," she whispered. The unwelcome idea of Otsana hauling a Hrōkr backpack across the mountains, its feet dragging in the dirt until the skin peeled while it whispered in her ear from a cauliflower head-stump, swam through True's dizzy mind.

They heaved the pack off one shoulder, chasing the shovel half-blind. The motion smacked to a halt, cold arms clamping around them from behind. *Fuck*, for a split second a hideous irrational fear of a mostly headless blond creature winked in their head. The knife sliced their skin. Stinging, not deadly. True planted a boot on the wall, twisting hard. Their captor struck the wall. The knife glanced their shoulder and sank deep into their pack. Blood joined the rain drenching their body. Just a surface wound, but the pack's strap sagged, cut clean.

A sopping dead man with a face of mottled yellow floundered their abandoned pack. Jonesy had shed his flannel, beneath he wore a thick linen, a watercolour bloodstain had pooled around the quarter-sized slit over his heart.

"You," they sputtered, but damned if they weren't at a loss for words and breath.

He held up a crudely bandaged hand with a dull-eyed smug grin. "Did you honestly think you were the first git to try backstabbing me? I'm a damn survivor, I will always make it through."

"And you will always be alone." They didn't bother mirroring that smug grin back at him. Lightning bathed the hall in blinding relief. There were no passageways branching off from the entrance, no place to go except out or through.

"The Faction must have some impressive resources hidden up here for you to abandon your home like that." They said, stalling. Jonesy always had liked to chat.

He scoffed. "No secret resources, we're just getting rid of resource wasters. Like you."

That hadn't lasted as long as they'd hoped.

Thunder rattled the fishery, and Jonesy surged. True recoiled to the catwalk. *Think*, they demanded, stumbling on the wavering grates. The rush of rain blinded them, and in the space between one blink and the next, a weight smacked them into the railing. The rusted bars groaned and snapped. Their pounding heart lurched into their throat. For an instant all that mattered, all that existed, was the yawning pit beneath them. Nothing between them and it.

Fucking heights. Why did it have to be heights. Sucking their organs back inside, they reeled away from the ledge on their knees. Could they even stand anymore? They had to.

True's pack sprawled on the catwalk between them, shovel swinging free of the ledge, out of reach. Otsana chased them out into the open air, Jonesy at her elbow. He feigned submission. And Otsana, she burned.

True lunged for the broken bar. It hung on by a scrap of rusted metal. Tearing it free, they thrust the jagged end at her. It popped, slid. Heat hit their face, for once not their own.

They wiped it away, breath hitching, and at the other end of the pole, Jonesy shivered over the broken pipe jutting from his gut. The betrayer, betrayed. Blood bubbled at his lips. Otsana grinned, winding the arm she'd used to propel him in front of her tighter, and pushed Jonesy.

Into True.

Off the catwalk.

27
The Throes of Death

Breathe. Ringing filled the inside of their head.

They gasped, sputtering against their waterlogged mask. Tore it off so all that choked them was the taste of their own blood and the rain hitting their teeth. The landings swam above them, bright splotches blotting chunks of the picture out the way the ringing blotted out crashes of thunder. Otsana stood aloof on the catwalk, peering down at them.

Warmth spread from their side, combatting the icy, numbing rain. It was almost pleasant. Almost. They let their eye close, head throbbing. Almost.

Shit, their stitches.

Their eye flew open, hand flying to the warm, wet injury. They sat up with a groan, only to collapse back down to their elbows, gasping and shivering. Stars burst in their head, over their vision. Hot pokers ripped at their chest and empty eye.

Shit, fuck, *ow*. They scrubbed their eye to combat stinging tears, if only because they needed clearer vision to see Otsana. Except she'd vanished from the catwalk. Probably coming to finish the job. They rocked to their side, clutching the torn path of new scar. Was that three broken ribs, or four? They swore they could feel the snapped ends scraping against each other when they moved. Blood drooled from somewhere behind their teeth. That wasn't great.

Legs sprawled over theirs, eyes open, bloodshot, was Jonesy. Railing bulging from his spine, a pillar aimed at the blackened sky, shards of fractured bone buckled outwards from its base.

They staggered to their feet, swayed in doubles. It was a straight shot to the open door, the lighter patch of grey in the distance acted as their guide.

Between flashes of lightning, a silhouette appeared I the door. Small, drenched. Radio started towards them, a bright streak of electricity lit the wide whites of its eyes.

Gone.

Never there.

True grabbed the slippery pipe and shook the body loose, bone scraping on the rusted metal. It let go with a squelch and flopped to the floor like a wet sandbag, landing in a puddle of its own fluids. Steam curled from the gaping wound, blood sloughing from the blunted point of the railing. It was unwieldy, it slipped in their grasp, but it was all they had. Their shovel hung from its clip four storeys up.

They peered up, skimming the flights of stairs and finding no glimpses of activity. Shrilling ringing bounced off the walls of their ear canals. They scanned the shadows for movement. The sensation of being watched set their hair on end. And yet, no sign of Otsana.

Warily, they backed away from the stairs and the corpse. Pressed a hand to the split as they went. Blood had soaked through to their coat. Oh well. Propping the rail on the wall, they fumbled with their sash and managed to get it up around the burst injury and cinched it tight. A sharp bite of pain bleached their vision white, then passed. Good enough. They'd get stitched back together when they made it back to the After Market. They were almost done. Almost. The bomb laying on the catwalk would have to suffice because they were not making it back up those stairs.

The downpour let up briefly as they limped further from the destroyed roof. The wind swirled around them, stealing their last remnants of body heat. A gust knocked them against the wall, rattling their broken bones.

"Ouch," they muttered under their breath. Still kind of hard to breathe. Kind of hurt a lot.

A figure appeared in the door. They hefted their makeshift weapon, ready.

"True!" It was Cal rushing towards them. There were scorch marks up his bare arms, a split-open bruise bubbled on his crown. Eliza trailed after him, arms empty of bombs and knives. "Suni's dead. They blew the Market. Where's Radio, Jonesy?"

"Dead, he—" a cough interrupted them, white-hot agony flash-bombed their body and left the taste of iron painted on the roof of their mouth. "He sold us out."

"You good?" Cal's voice sounded wavy.

"Mmhmm." The fishery had tipped on its side again. The ear ringing blew up to an entire brass section over which the heard faint strains of cursing. Eliza gripped their chin and forced them to look up at her. Two Eliza's stared back down at them, the crazy in her eyes a touch intense. Too much like Allsaint.

"You ruined my stitches," she tutted.

"Not now." Cal smacked her hand away. Bending, he looped True's arm over his shoulders.

"Ribs," True gasped as blinding waves wracked them, "ribs."

Cal stumbled, footing lost on the rain-slick floor. Cleared his throat. Lost his hold.

True hadn't heard the knife slide in. But they heard the tearing flesh when Cal collapsed, a midnight shade of red sloughing from his open neck.

Eliza blinked down at him.

True pivoted to catch a glancing blow with their pipe. A sneer flitted over Otsana's harsh expression. She butted what was left of True's nose, slamming a shock of static across their brain.

Groaning, they struggled to keep their feet under them. They slipped on the blood. Cal's blood. He lay face-down in it, scarred hand stretched out over Eliza's foot, as if he'd been reaching for help. Unmistakably dead. Hysterics clawed at True's throat.

"What are you laughing about?" Otsana snarled, seizing the pipe and slamming them into the wall with it. All the air vacated their lungs with a crunch.

Scraping in a breath, they said, "You fucked up."

A streak of pale skin and dark hair slammed into Otsana. Someone's skull cacked on the cement. Devoid of the brief support from Otsana pinning them to the wall. True sagged to the floor. Chest cavity filled with angry wasps, they could do little else but watch the fight.

Eliza came up on top. Fists clawed into Otsana's hair. Gone was any semblance of sanity. She was feral. She was furious. She slammed Otsana's head into the floor. Again, again. Screaming while she did.

A dark stain bloomed on the wet concrete. Otsana's knife lay abandoned, just within reach of her searching fingers. Lurching to their feet, True limped for the knife.

"Eliza!" the warning fell on deaf ears, punctuated by the sharp abrupt gasp of a woman with a knife plunged into her gut.

Blood fountained over Tosana. It shrouded her, coating her eyes and everything around them. Steam gathered where hot blood struck cold floor. With a guttural cry, Eliza wrenched Otsana's arm, knife and all, from the gaping wound. Bit off two fingers. She dove into Otsana's scream, sinking her jagged teeth into cheek muscle and ripped it free.

True straggled closer to the fight, using the bloodied pipe as a crutch.

Otsana heaved Eliza off. Brandishing the knife in her mangled hand, but the blade didn't get the opportunity to bite flesh. With a solid thunk, her head whipped back. An impression of the broken handrail denting the side of her blood-soaked skull. She deflated. Another crack of the pipe crunched her eye socket. By the time she hit the ground she was limp, lifeless.

They kicked away the knife for good measure. Knelt in the spreading pool of blood to get a better look at Eliza's damage.

She swayed, hands pressed loosely to the stab wound. It dumped her life out in pulses, her own heartbeat jettisoning blood from the injury.

"It's better this way," she said, glassy unfocused eyes fixed on Cal's body. Her breaths came in lurches that rattled her chest. "I never wanted that stupid disease to get me."

Her hands abandoned the pretence of holding anything in. It was too late, there was too much blood. Steam rose around her, a ghost twining itself around the remains of its body a final time. And the body sank, exhausted at last.

True closed her eyes.

It was time to go.

The storm, for all its shrieking and downpour, had not scrubbed the fish odor from the island. True hobbled from the fishery and spotted the lump at the island-side base of the bridge. Radio had laid the final bomb. Radio itself was nowhere to be seen.

The storm battered True, livid and writhing. They scanned the far bank for glimpses of Radio as they limped for the bridge. Flickers of orange peeked between the trees, phantoms of the last After Market. Between flashes of lightning and fire, marched the Red Faction.

A mob much larger than the one that had marched out of the fishery not too long ago teemed in the street. Both the hunting party and the shadow killers at the base of the bridge returning home. The head of the pack set foot on the bridge, cutting off all escape.

Lightning cracked, transforming night to day and carrying with it a final, desperate idea. True cast their gaze over the far bank once more.

There, in the clump of brush where they had waited earlier, a form, Radio.

Crashing to their knees by the bomb, they freed the bottle from their belt. Popped the lid. Dumped half the contents on the bomb, then heaved to their feet and hobbled as fast as they could manage toward the fishery.

The bottle coughed the last of its content midway between building and bridge. They cast it aside, dug their lighter from the coat pocket. If ever the needed a lighter that sparked in the wind, it was now.

The mob reached the halfway point of the bridge, by now the lead must have spotted True, but they made no effort to hurry. The troupe carried on its steady march. The only way off the island was through its mass. What was one lone scavenger compared to their war party? The Red Faction had already won.

The bridge groaned as it took on the full mass of the mob. A groan the Red Faction would hear again and again as its numbers grew. As its message spread. As it shaped the world into what it should be instead of what it was.

The tail of the mob stepped foot on the bridge as the head was mid-step off, and in that brief moment when the entirety of the Red Faction stood on the barnacled wooden bridge, the scavenger knelt and touched their flame to the fuel.

Fire flare, scorching an unstoppable path toward the Faction. Spark, flash, *boom*.

28
The Way the World Burns

Smoke in their mouth. They were alive. They were alive?

They coughed, an earthquake shattered them inside out. Too agonizing to scream. Screaming would hurt. Instead, they laid very still, and gulped oleos air like a fish plucked from water.

Brain felt popped. Nothing in their ears, not even that infernal ringing. They were deaf now, they were pretty sure. Not that it mattered, their only friend was mute. Not that that mattered, they were dead. When, not if. Brain damaged, broken boned, bleeding out. Their best chance at medical supplies burning in the decimated building shell behind them. The only way off the island utterly destroyed, its carnage littered the island and ocean, little fires consuming the debris. Not a single survivor.

That half-assed plan had worked. All those factioneers, blown to pieces with the bridge. They'd known that rickety thing would kill someone. A weak laugh slithered past their lips. Now they were trapped, doomed by its absence.

The stilted laughter grew stronger. Inside joke. Inside hysterics. They always had been prone to gallows humour.

A pebble struck their cheek. It kind of surprised them that they had a cheek. Every bit of exposed skin felt singed.

Thok. Another pebble bounced off their forehead. What the fuck. They rolled to one side, body spasming in protest. Forced their eye to focus. Vision wasn't doing so hot. Moving turned the island into smears of light and shadow. They wiped char and gunk from their face.

Reaching back, they touched an aching spot on their head. Their scalp felt spongy. Then again, they were soaked head to toe. They picked out a shard of gravel that had tried to embed itself. It came away off-white, smeared with red. They turned it, squinting at the porous edges and smooth sides.

Was that a piece of their fucking skull?

Some part of them that wasn't completely out of it gagged. They dropped the shard. A spray of pebbles peppered their face.

"Fuck off—"

Their anger falling out as they looked up. Into the gaps flooded terror, pure and gut-wrenching. It hit hard, blacked out their vison as they lurched to their hands and knees.

A demon of red sulfur and volcanic glass arced her knife at their last remaining eye.

A fury of black crashed into her at the last instant.

Black and pink and white and red and torn rags and old scars and piebald hair and the knife and Radio and Otsana.

Not escaped.

Not dead.

The gravel under their shoes skittering in every direction. Radio blocked Otsana's knife arm and twisted it behind her. Quick, sure, except for a drag in its step. The knife stuck hilt-up in the dirt. Otsana's mangled face, warped and half-sunken, heaved with bitter anger. She met True's stare. Held it as she bucked hard, slamming her head square into Radio's face. It staggered. She slipped free, shoulder slopped in a wrong way.

She dropped, spinning, shin crashed into Radio's knee and sent it sprawling.

In a wild hurricane of limbs, she had the knife and launched for True. Radio tore her off-course. It threw up its arms in the nick of time. The blade pierced clean through.

True lurched to their feet. Ignored the wildfire pain consuming every fiber of their body. Bones grinding and popping. World turning out-of-control circles. One more step, they lied to a knee that ballooned and mushed at the same time, like the time-bomb milk cartons. Please, they begged, one more minute, please. They had nothing left to trade.

Ahead of them, Radio heaved Otsana off. Abused metal snapped, blade abandoned in its arm. It rolled to its feet, Otsana mere seconds behind it. She stumbled, empty-handed. Her back to True. Within reach.

Radio caught sight of them, something unreadable flickering across its face. Otsana seized the distraction. She lunged. True lunged with her. They wrapped around her as she beat Radio's arms. The deflected blow bounced her back into True's grasp.

No time to think. They crushed her close to them and plunged their hand into her smashed eye socket. Molten blood erupted around their fingers. Soft tissue squelching under nails. Otsana writhed apoplectically. Drove her elbow into their broken ribs. Bucked her head back again, again, desperate to escape the thing clawing its way inside.

True gave a final shove, felt a pop, and that was it. Mid-breath, mid-thrash, mid-fight she ceased. She crumpled, mangled skull sliding off True's hand. Her remaining volcanic eye now dull. Dead. For good this time.

Vertigo washed over True, threatening to take them down, too. Fighting for breath, they lifted their gaze to Radio.

"No." The pleas caught on the torn edges of their throat. Radio unstuck its skewered arm and freed the blade from its neck. Dark arterial blood flooded from the gash. No, that wasn't *fair*.

They dragged one foot toward it, but that as all. That was the last of their strength. Milk carton knee buckled. They crumpled in slow motion. Trying to stretch out and out and out, to resist the impossible weight of gravity.

Radio managed to stagger across the lake of gore, four uneasy steps exhausted it. It slumped down next to them and rested its head on True's shoulder. They folded it into them, needed to hold it, and to feel its pulse on their cold skin.

The rain had let up in the wake of the explosion, as if evaporated by the sheet heat of their destruction. Only a light sprinkle remained to soothe the damage. Patches of night skin peeking between the thinning clouds, filled to the brim with brilliant ribboning northern lights and glittering stars. True watched the reflection in Radio's eyes, then tilted their chin to watch the soft green glimmers trailing down to meet them.

"Did I ever tell you I love the stars?" they whispered.

Radio Silent squeezed their hand. Once, twice.

It wasn't such a bad way to die.

Acknowledgements

Thank you to my sister, Sasha, for being so supportive and for reading the terrible first draft of pretty much anything I put in front of her. It takes a lot of patience to put up with that much incoherence.

Thank you also to my parents, Deborah and Ernest, and my brother, Kohen, for your love and support, and for putting up with my hermeticism and allergy to texting. I love you all, I'm just oblivious to the passage of time, forgive me.

Big huge thank you to my beta readers: Adam Pacholik, A. Jani Reitsm, Ashleigh Mattern, and Naz! Without you there would be many more plot holes, weird grammar, and characters mistaken for cats.

Finally thank you to God for not smiting me or my computer (and many other great things).